Bobblehead Beatdown

a story of courage and friendship
in youth sports

by Bo Rush

Earth's Future Publishing

Dedicated to my father and to my three sons

ISBN 978-0-9644101-5-2

Published by Earth's Future Publishing

CONTENTS

Bobblehead Beatdown

Bobblehead Touchdown

The score is tied at 24. The clock ticks down... 15, 14, 13, 12... The bobblehead quarterback's helmet bounces up and down as he barks out signals.

11, 10, 9... He drops back to pass, his wooden face unmoved by the oncoming blitz.

8, 7, 6... He rifles the ball downfield just as a pair of snarling linebackers pancake him.

The sacked quarterback's head shoots up high into the air, then springs back down to his shoulders.

The wide receiver is open in the end zone. He reaches up, but the football is spiraling five feet above him.

The receiver's bobblehead suddenly springs up from his shoulders, way, way, up. Five feet up! The football hits his helmet and falls into the receiver's hands!

Touchdown!

Zach Fargo cracked open an eye to look at the line of bobblehead football players on the shelf next to his bed.

They were all motionless, lifeless. Why wouldn't they be?

Zach laughed at himself for even feeling the need to check. After all, it was just the same old dream he'd had for years. His bobblehead collection coming to life, playing in a real football game, always using their springy heads to make some incredible play.

He glanced at the clock on the desk, the desk that was supposed to be a study desk, but was always too cluttered with sports magazines and dirty jerseys – 8:30. Way too early to get up on Saturday.

Zach's head sank back down into the pillow. Maybe he could continue that dream and catch the post-game interviews.

8:30! Zach suddenly shot up out of bed, banging his knee against the wooden bedpost.

8:30! Football practice was at 9! Not just any practice, but his first practice in the youth majors, the 11-13 year old league! His first practice for the Lightning!

2

Zach pulled a jersey over his head. How could he have overslept today of all days?! He grabbed his helmet and cleats and yanked open the bedroom door.

Zach suddenly stopped and looked back at the bobbleheads on the shelf by his bed. That *was* an amazing catch he just saw in his dream.

"If only I could use my head like those bobbleheads!" Zach laughed to himself. "I could be a great football player!"

-2-
First Practice

The other Lightning players were already loosening up, tossing footballs and joking around, when Zach raced across the field on his bike. He skidded to a stop, quickly pulling his helmet off the handlebars.

"Nice of you to make it, Fargo!" Chris Rivera laughed and threw a football at Zach.

Zach, still holding the helmet, had to use it as a shield to knock the ball away. "How early did you get here, Chris? Real early, I hope, since you need the extra practice!"

Which wasn't true, since Chris was the best football player he knew. Zach picked up the pigskin and tossed it back to his best friend, but it sailed over Chris's outstretched hand.

"Good thing you're not our QB, Zach."

"Yeah. You do the throwing and I'll do the catching."

Chris retrieved the ball and cocked his arm to fire it to Zach. A whistle pierced the air. All the boys stopped their warm-ups and turned to see

Coach MacDuffy standing with his hands on his hips at mid-field.

Chris tucked the football and grinned at Zach, "Ready to rock and roll, amigo?"

"Ready?" Zach nodded and smiled back. "I've been waiting my whole life for this day!"

Quarterback to Wide Receiver

Which wasn't exactly true. Zach didn't even know what football was until he was four years old. And his dream of playing in the youth majors wasn't really a dream until two years ago. His first year of organized football in the peewee league.

Two years ago Zach was on the Zephyrs, and the team was so pitiful that the coach actually had Zach playing quarterback. Which wasn't as ridiculous as it sounded because peewee football features a lot more running than passing. And running was Zach's thing. His dad always said he could outrun a cheetah, if they were both wearing cleats.

A couple of the linemen on the Zephyrs, twin brothers and twice Zach's size, were jealous of the rookie quarterback. Max and Dalton Schwartz secretly teased Zach every chance they got, saying the only reason he was quarterback was because his dad was the coach.

That part was true. Zach's dad was the volunteer coach. But that's not why Zach was the starting quarterback. He had proven time and again in wind sprints that he had the fastest wheels on the team. That kind of blazing speed would mean touchdowns once the season started.

But that didn't seem to matter to the annoying Schwartz twins. They kept up a side conversation in the huddle at practice while Zach was trying to call plays.

"Alright, guys. Six veer bootleg shuffle."

Max Schwartz laughed, "What's Peyton Manning whining about now?"

"Probably that he needs his diaper changed," sneered Dalton.

Zach didn't tell his dad about the daily taunts in the huddle. He figured if he was going to run the offense, he needed to act like it didn't bother him.

The Schwartz twins' complaint – that Zach was the starting quarterback because his dad was the coach – was proven wrong two days before the season opener. That's when a new kid showed up at practice.

This new kid had just moved to Westridge from Texas. He was nine, just like Zach, but was a head taller. And when Coach Fargo had the team run wind sprints, Zach found himself in the unusual position of eating a teammate's dust.

That was how he met Chris Rivera. And that was the day Zach became a wide receiver instead of a quarterback.

-4-
Big Shoes to Fill

Lightning Coach Charlie MacDuffy had won more games than he could remember in his 27 years as a youth football coach. The occasional losses he never seemed able to forget.

The Lightning had been champs of the majors the last three years. They didn't lose a single game during that span – a 21 game winning streak!

Coach Mac, as everyone called him, didn't like to waste words. That's why he always wore a whistle around his neck. He also didn't like to waste time. That's why, as he stood at midfield with his hands on his hips, he looked like a man expecting bad news.

But the bad news didn't come, because the 16 Lightning players speedily formed a half circle around the coach. Coach Mac's eyes looked over the boys who were standing like soldiers at attention. He nodded approvingly.

"I see you know how to huddle up. Let's see if you can play football."

That was it. That was Coach Mac's introduction to this new group of 11 year olds, none of whom had played in the youth majors before that September morning. He blew his whistle and had the boys stretching, doing pushups, and running wind sprints for the rest of the practice session.

Most teams in the majors have a mix of 11, 12, and 13 year olds. That way, five or six players move on to high school ball every year and are replaced by boys coming up from the peewees. Teams don't have to replace entire rosters and suffer through winless seasons.

But for the past three years the Lightning had a unique group of boys. They came into the league as 11 year olds and swept through their first season undefeated. The next two years saw the same success.

That talented group of boys won three championships and 21 games in a row! Now they were working out with the Westridge High team.

Zach, Chris, and the other rookies knew about the previous Lightning teams. They knew they had big shoes to fill.

The Lightning had only two players returning from last year's squad. Dylan Yeager was a stocky two-way tackle who could open up gaping holes on offense and stuff the run when playing defense. Jared Greenberg was a speedy running back and shutdown corner.

Such a major rebuilding effort like the one facing the Lightning this season would worry most coaches. If it bothered Coach Mac, no one could tell. He just kept blowing his whistle and silently watching the workout routines with his hands on his hips.

None of the 16 Lightning players said a word. Exhausted and dripping with sweat, they didn't have the strength to talk. Zach felt like his leg muscles were on fire as the boys lined up again and again to sprint down the field.

Peewee practices had been nothing like this. It seemed like Zach's dad had spent most of the time showing the little kids where to stand and which direction to run. The Zephyrs hadn't spent entire practices getting in shape. If they had, most of the team probably wouldn't have shown up again.

Coach Mac didn't care if you never returned to practice. He knew he couldn't win games with players who weren't fully committed to football.

His grueling early season conditioning practices achieved two goals – weak players quit and those that stuck it out were stronger and in better physical shape than anyone else in the league.

Coach Mac's whistle blew a final time and the 16 boys wearily huddled up around him.

"I know that wasn't much fun, boys. I respect your toughness and I appreciate you not complaining. See you Tuesday at four. Who knows, maybe I'll let you actually touch a football then."

Coach Mac gave them a nod, then turned and walked away. Zach, Chris and the other newcomers looked at each other in disbelief. They had just spent two hours at their first youth majors football practice and hadn't touched a football the entire time!

-5-
Boot Camp

Zach learned a lot about mental and physical toughness during those first two weeks of football practice. His whole body ached. Muscles he didn't even know existed screamed with pain. He felt like an 80 year old man getting out of bed in the morning.

A hot shower seemed to loosen the muscles up a bit. But when Zach rolled his bike out of the garage to ride to school, it was all he could do to lift his right leg up over the seat. The bike wobbled as Zach started off, pedaling slowly, grunting in pain.

It helped Zach to know he wasn't alone. Fifteen other boys in the neighborhood were going through the same torture. By the time he pedaled to the corner where he always met Chris, Zach's muscles were warmed up and he was feeling almost normal. He sat on his bike and laughed as his buddy pedaled stiff-legged toward him.

"I didn't know we signed up for Marine boot camp," Chris grimaced.

"Don't worry," Zach responded, still laughing. "After a while the pain starts to feel normal."

Which was true. About the time the pain did begin to feel normal, it started to slowly fade away. At the end of those first two weeks of practice, the boys not only were pain free, but stronger physically and tougher mentally than they'd ever been in their lives.

At least 14 of the original 16 Lightning players were stronger. Two of the 11 year olds had quit before the first week had ended.

6

The Playbook

The way Coach Mac was always blasting that whistle of his and demanding his players to push past their own limits, it might seem like he didn't really like his job. The truth was, he loved it.

And when he saw his players finally toughening up, the workout drills stopped. It was time to open up the playbook and begin preparing for the season opener.

Getting his players into superior shape was one reason for the incredible success Coach Mac had in youth football. The other reason was his playbook and what it represented – which was Coach Mac's amazing mind. He was known across the state as a football genius.

Opposing coaches spent hours analyzing Lightning plays and trying to figure out ways to stop them – usually without success. It seemed like Coach Mac had included so many options into each play that it was impossible to prepare for them all. Even local high school coaches copied some of his most successful offensive and defensive formations.

There was only one copy of that playbook, and it never left the hands of Coach Mac. Rumor had it that he slept with it under his pillow, although Mrs. MacDuffy insisted that wasn't true. She said he kept it on the nightstand next to their bed so he could add to it if he dreamed up a new play.

Over the years, Coach Mac had received offers to coach at the high school level, but he turned them all down. There was something about being able to lead young boys, to get them to play the right way before they started developing bad habits. That's what kept Coach Mac in youth football.

The hundreds of boys Coach Mac put through his demanding drills in the past 27 years might not have realized it at the time, but they were the lucky ones. Coach Mac helped them become talented football players and excellent young men.

Coach Mac saw Chris's running speed on display during the two weeks of workout drills. Even speedy Jared Greenberg couldn't match Chris's long stride that ate up yardage like a top fuel dragster devours asphalt.

Most youth majors teams feature athletic quarterbacks who can outrun defenses. However, the strength of Chris's right arm and the laser-like accuracy of his passes were amazing for an 11 year old. It only took ten minutes watching Chris throw passes for Coach Mac to name him as the Lightning's new quarterback.

"Nice arm, kid. You're our QB."

Chris looked surprised by the coach's matter-of-fact announcement. He looked to Zach to make sure he'd heard right. Zach grinned and slapped Chris's back.

"Alright, Chris!"

Coach Mac developed plenty of talented quarterbacks during his long coaching career, but the prospect of a dual threat QB like Chris had the veteran coach quickly sketching new plays in his playbook.

"Great..." Chris stammered, unsure what to say. "Uh, you know, Coach, Zach was my main receiver on the Zephyrs."

Coach Mac looked up from his playbook at Chris, then silently sized up Zach. "We'll see." He returned his attention to his playbook.

Zach looked at Chris and nodded. That was all he wanted – to be given a chance at earning a spot as one of the Lightning's starting wide receivers.

7

Dreaming of Football Plays

Most football coaches give their plays coded names like "42 Dive Option Left" or "Sam Blast Left 44". Each number and word tells the "who, what, and where" of the play.

"Wing Right 24 Dive" means the offense lines up in a wing formation, with both running backs on the right side of the quarterback. The tailback runs the ball through the four hole, which is between the right guard and tackle.

Plays are sent to the quarterback from the sideline. A coach or back-up quarterback uses hand signals to show the play. Frequently, the starting quarterback wears a wristband that lists all the plays.

Coach Mac had invented hundreds of plays during his career. But he wasn't the only one on the Lightning who spent time dreaming up new plays.

Zach had been doing it since his first year in the peewees. He drew X's and O's on sheets of paper to represent the offense and defense, then sketched pass routes, blocking assignments, and blitz packages that he imagined would be successful on the field. Since he didn't understand the complex play-calling codes, Zach gave his plays simple names like "Banana Pass" and "Wiggle Worm".

Zach had created well over a hundred football plays. He kept them in a three-ring binder in the top drawer of his bedroom study desk. When it was time to do homework, he found himself doodling plays in the margins of his papers. He erased those before turning in the assignments, but not before copying any particularly interesting ones.

Whenever Zach sketched out a new play, he saw it unfold in his imagination like it was happening in a real game...

The Dallas quarterback calls the Banana Pass, then drops back and surveys the field. His receivers zigzag toward the end zone as the crowd roars. The quarterback heaves a rocket to number 89, who clutches the ball as he crosses the goal line...

In his imagination, Zach's plays almost always resulted in six points.

No one knew about Zach's interest in making up football plays – not his parents, certainly not his little sister Kate, not even Chris. It wasn't that he didn't want to share the plays. He just didn't know if they were good enough.

After all, it was basically impossible to test them in the cul-de-sac when Chris came over or on the playground after school. Zach needed two whole teams to see if the plays would really work like they did in his imagination.

So he just kept filling up the binder with his dreams.

Big Brother

Zach's dad had found out over the summer that the satellite dish company he worked for was going out of business.

But Mr. Fargo never acted like anything was the least bit different after he lost his job. His family's health and happiness remained the most important things in his life. He was as positive as always, whether he was sending out job applications, helping Kate with her math homework, or fixing the toilet leak in the basement.

The only times Zach sensed the money worries his parents were going through were when he overheard their whispered conversations. One of those times, Kate snuck up behind Zach as he stood in the hallway outside their parents' closed bedroom door.

"Spying on Mom and Daddy?"

Zach was so startled he nearly jumped out of his skin. He took Kate by the arm and led her away from the door. She could tell something was up just by the way Zach didn't seem to be mad at her.

"What's wrong? What were Mom and Daddy saying in there, Zach?"

"Nothing's wrong, Kate. Hey, do you want to go downstairs and help me build a fort with the couch cushions?"

Kate's face lit up. She grabbed her big brother's hand and eagerly dashed downstairs.

A love of sports wasn't the only thing Zach had learned from his father. He'd learned it was important to try to spare others from worry.

A New Coach

Zach's dad decided not to coach the peewee Zephyrs this season. The Lightning's games were on Saturdays, just like the Zephyrs, and Mr. Fargo didn't want to miss a single second of his son's first season in the youth majors.

He frequently stopped by the Lakeview Middle School field where Coach Mac held Lightning practices, and always gave Zach a thumbs-up when he caught a pass from Chris or cleared the way for a long run with a crushing block.

Zach could tell that his dad missed coaching football. Zach thought that coaching might keep his dad's mind off the unpleasant fact that he hadn't found a job that would pay the family's bills.

Despite every thumbs-up at practice, Zach could tell that his dad was struggling to keep up his positive spirit. That's why he approached Coach Mac after practice one week before the season opener.

"Here, let me help you, Coach Mac." Zach gathered up a half dozen footballs and dropped them into a mesh bag for the coach to take to his car.

When Zach finished collecting all the balls, Coach Mac closed his playbook and reached for the bag.

"I can carry it for you." Zach swung the bag of balls over his shoulder.

Coach Mac nodded and started for the parking lot. He popped the trunk of his sedan so Zach could stash the mesh bag inside.

"Thanks, kid." Coach Mac slammed the trunk and walked to the driver's door. Zach followed him.

"Could you use some help, Coach?"

"You already helped me." He opened the car door.

"I mean, regularly. Like at practices and games."

Coach Mac turned to Zach with a puzzled look. "What are you talking about, Zach?"

"I, um, I was just thinking, that my dad, um, well…" Zach fidgeted nervously and stared down at his shoelaces.

"What about your dad?"

Zach looked up, blurting out, "He could help you!"

Coach Mac still didn't understand what Zach was getting at.

"With anything you need help with! He's a coach, too, you know. He coached the Zephyrs and we won the Peewee Bowl last year! He's a great guy and I know you'd really like him!"

Coach Mac was silent for a long moment as he thought about Zach's unexpected offer.

"That's quite a recommendation." He reached out and put a hand on Zach's shoulder. "If your dad is anything like you, I'd love to have him help the team."

Zach's face lit up. "Thanks, Coach Mac! My dad and I will see you at practice Tuesday!"

Coach Mac smiled softly as he watched Zach race full-speed back to the field to scoop up his helmet, then veer toward the bicycle rack where Chris waited.

"What'd he say?" Chris asked as Zach hopped onto his bike.

"He said yes! Dad's gonna be so happy! I can't wait to tell him!"

The two boys, still wearing their practice gear – shoulder pads, cleats, and helmets – started pedaling home.

"Don't you wish the first game was tomorrow, Zach?"

"Yeah, I don't think I can stand to wait a whole week!" Zach replied.

As Chris turned right, Zach turned left onto the cul-de-sac where he lived.

"Want to come over tomorrow and throw the ball?" called Zach.

"Definitely."

Chris gave a wave. As he pedaled away, he turned and shouted. "Hey, Zach, which thing do you think your dad will be happier about?"

"Huh?

"Him being a coach or you being our wide receiver!"

Zach and Chris had spent hours before and after every practice working on pass routes. They perfected their timing so that, even before Zach had made his final cut, Chris would zip the ball and Zach would turn and catch it in full stride.

They even developed their own form of communication. If Zach saw that his planned route was clogged with defenders, he would give his shoulder pads a tiny shake and Chris instantly knew what adjustment to make to his throw.

Zach's speed and sure hands had not gone unnoticed at practice. Coach Mac had Zach working with the Lightning's first team!

-10-
Bad News for Zach

Zach's mom was removing Buffalo wings from a takeout box and putting them on plates on the table as Zach entered the kitchen from the garage.

"Hey, mom!" Zach took off his helmet and kicked off his cleats. "Wow, Buffalo wings!" Zach was surprised to see the wings because his family hadn't ordered food from restaurants much since his dad had lost his job.

"Zach!" Mr. Fargo called out with a big grin. "C'mon, sit down! We're celebrating!"

"Wash your hands first, sweetheart," his mom reminded Zach.

Zach washed speedily, trying to figure out how his family already knew about the great news he was planning on surprising them with.

Kate was sitting beside her mother and father at the table when Zach sat down.

"Did Coach Mac call or something?" Zach couldn't hide his smile.

"Coach Mac? No, why?" his dad responded.

"Then how do you guys know about it?"

"The company called your father this afternoon," Zach's mom explained. "It's a tremendous opportunity for your father." She squeezed her husband's hand and smiled at him.

"What are you talking about? What company?" Zach asked.

"His new job!" Kate squealed.

Mr. Fargo answered, "The satellite company I interviewed with last month wants to hire me!"

"Isn't it wonderful?" Zach's mom gushed.

"That's great!" Zach gave his father a high five across the table. "I've got some good news, too!"

"Really? What's that?" His dad was still grinning broadly as he tore into a wing.

"Coach Mac said you could be an assistant coach for the Lightning! He said you could start right away, at our next practice!"

Mr. Fargo's grin faded. He put down the wing and glanced at his wife, who was also no longer smiling.

"What's wrong?" Zach looked from his dad to his mom, then back to his dad. "Don't you want to be a coach again, Dad?"

"I'd like that more than anything, Zach. It's just that…"

"Your father has to attend training for three months in Connecticut."

The news stunned Zach. "You mean, you're gonna move there? Without us?!"

His father nodded.

"When?!"

"I fly there on Monday."

"But… What about the games? Are you going to come back on the weekends?"

"The airline tickets are too expensive, honey," his mom said gently.

"I wish I could, son. But they said I'd be working weekends, too. I promise I'll be back by Thanksgiving."

"But, the season will be over!" Zach protested.

"I know, but Mom's going to record all the games for me. I'll get to watch them in Connecticut!"

Zach stared at the uneaten Buffalo wings on his plate and blinked back sudden hot tears.

"I'm gonna miss you so much, Daddy!" Kate jumped into her father's lap, crying.

Mrs. Fargo circled around behind Zach and hugged him.

"It's going to be hard for all of us, Zach," she said softly.

Mr. Fargo reached across the table, putting his hand on Zach's. "We have to be strong for each other, son."

Zach didn't see how he could play all season without his dad cheering him on like he had always done. He didn't see how he could even live with his dad gone.

But, he knew his dad was right. With his father away in Connecticut, Zach would be the only man at home. He had to be strong, starting now.

-11-
Two Lucky Boys

The next day, Zach and Chris were jumping their bikes off a ramp they had built on the sidewalk in front of Zach's house. They took turns racing at full speed, hitting the ramp, landing with fingers tightly crossed, then whooping loudly and turning to do it again.

"Watch this!" Chris yelled as he crouched with his feet on the seat. He hit the edge of the ramp, veered wildly and crashed.

Zach sped over to him. "Man! What a wipeout! That was amazing!"

"Thanks," Chris groaned as he got to his feet, checking to make sure he was all in one piece.

Zach's dad drove up in his pick-up just as Chris picked up his bike.

"Whoa!" Mr. Fargo said. "You okay, Chris?"

"Yeah, I landed on the grass," Chris answered. "But this wheel doesn't look so good."

Zach's dad looked at the bent front wheel of Chris's bike. "Yeah, you won't be riding on this anymore."

"Can't we bend it back into place?" Zach asked.

"No, the wheel will have to be replaced," Mr. Fargo answered.

Chris's face looked as crushed as his ruined bike.

"You can use my bike, Chris," Zach offered.

"I have a better idea," said Mr. Fargo. "Let's stop by the bike shop and see if they have a replacement." He loaded Chris's bike in the back of the pick-up.

At the bike store, when the clerk pointed to a brand new wheel and said it cost 65 bucks, Zach could see Chris's face fill with despair.

"Maybe your mom could call and give them her credit card," Mr. Fargo suggested.

"No," Chris answered quietly and looked toward the door. "I'll get it some other time."

Mr. Fargo's pick-up cruised along a dusty street lined with warehouses. Although Chris was a frequent guest at the Fargo home, Zach had never been to Chris's house. Chris pointed to a small house where he and his mom lived. Parked in front was a rusted white minivan with one black door on the driver's side.

"Thanks for the ride," Chris said as he reached to lift his bike out of the bed of the pick-up.

Mr. Fargo nodded, but was looking at Chris's house. The paint had peeled off long ago and the tiny front porch sagged to the left.

"Say, Chris, why don't you leave the bike in the truck?"

Chris looked puzzled.

"He needs it to get to school, Dad," Zach explained.

"He's not going anywhere on that thing. And I have a friend who might have an extra wheel."

Chris's face lit up. "Really?"

Mr. Fargo nodded.

"That'd be great!" Chris pumped Mr. Fargo's hand, then turned and dashed to his house, calling over his shoulder. "See ya, Zach!"

"Dad?" asked Zach.

"Yeah, Zach?"

"Who's your friend?"

"Hmm?"

"Who's your friend with the extra bike wheel?"

Mr. Fargo just smiled and put his arm around his son. He didn't have to answer because Zach knew there wasn't a friend with a spare wheel.

When Zach's dad saw Chris's rundown home, he figured it might be a long time before Chris could afford to replace that wheel. So, on the way home, he and Zach returned to the bike shop and bought the 65 dollar wheel for Chris's bike.

There was just one thing Mr. Fargo made Zach promise – not to tell Chris where the wheel really came from.

"But, Dad, isn't that lying?"

"No, Zach. That's just doing the right thing."

Chris's eyes grew big when they delivered the repaired bike.

"Wow! Your friend had a brand-new wheel!"

"We got lucky," Mr. Fargo replied.

"Yeah," Zach smiled proudly at his dad. "We got real lucky."

-12-
A New Bobblehead

Zach's dad had an early flight Monday morning. While the airport van waited out front, he slipped into Zach's bedroom and put a present on the desk next to the bed.

When Zach woke up two hours later he found the gift – a new bobblehead. Next to the bobblehead Zach found a note from his father.

> Dear Zach,
> The next three months will be a challenge for us. I'm thankful I have a son I can count on.
> Love,
> Dad

Zach tapped the top of bobblehead's helmet. As the plastic head bounced up and down, tears rolled down Zach's cheeks. He didn't know if he could survive without his dad for three months.

-13-
Starting Line-ups

At Tuesday's practice, Coach Mac announced the starting line-ups for Saturday's season opener against the Scorpions.

On offense, Chris was joined in the backfield by offensive captain Jared Greenberg at running back and William Chen in the slot. William was a small and shifty runner with a knack for finding the open spots in a defense's secondary.

The tight end was Kelvin Jones, by far the tallest player on the Lightning and a perfect target for the lob pass. Zach was paired at wide receiver with Connor Shaw.

While Zach had sure hands and ran exact pass routes, Connor frequently dropped easy passes and forgot where he was supposed to run. But every time Coach Mac was ready to move him to back-up tackle, Connor would make a circus catch that no one else could have made.

The offensive line was anchored by 13 year old Dylan Yeager at left tackle. Dylan started at tackle for the previous two undefeated Lightning teams, and all the other boys looked up to him as a leader.

Luis Chavez was the smallest player on the team, but Coach Mac put him at right tackle because he was tough and fearless. Luis easily won every push-up contest, and he was the only player who had knocked over Dylan in blocking drills.

Two former Zephyrs, Austin Harrison and Parker Coates, were the starting guards. They were both big, strong boys, but they couldn't have been more different off the field.

Austin was quiet and serious. He'd been playing the piano since he was five, and always won all the talent shows at school. Parker was an easy-going kid who had moved to Westridge from a farm. Parker couldn't play the piano, but he knew a lot about raising pigs.

The center was Owen Carlson, a former soccer goalie who was playing his first year of organized football. Owen's strong right leg meant he was also the Lightning's new kicker.

Dylan, the Lightning's defensive captain, was joined on the front four by Luis, Austin, and Parker. Chris, the best athlete on the team, was named as the starting middle linebacker, flanked by Kelvin Jones and Lucas Higney. Lucas was a curly-haired joker who liked to sneak up on people, then scream that he was a superhero as he jumped on their backs.

The cornerbacks were Jared Greenberg and William Chen, with Marcus Newman at strong safety. Marcus was a competitive wrestler. When he tackled someone on the football field, they never got away.

Coach Mac named Zach as the Lightning's starting free safety. Zach was happy about it, but he felt bad for Curtis Briggs. Curtis was the only member of the Lightning who didn't have a starting job on either the offense or defense.

No one knew exactly why Curtis was even on the team. He was small and skinny and wore thick glasses that he was always pushing back on his nose. And he had never played football before this season.

Lucas had said that Curtis was actually a math genius. They went to the same school, so maybe it was true. Although, when Lucas said something, you never knew whether to believe it or not.

As much as Zach loved playing wide receiver, especially with the timing he and Chris had developed, there was something special about playing free safety. Lining up behind the other defenders, he could see the whole play developing, then use his instincts to go to the ball.

Zach had intercepted 12 passes last year for the Zephyrs, returning four of them for touchdowns. Of course, picking off those passes had been easy because peewee quarterbacks stared at their receivers before throwing the ball. All Zach had to do was follow the quarterback's eyes and cut in front of the receiver.

He would find out on Saturday that intercepting passes in the youth majors was a whole different ballgame.

-14-
Seven Touchdowns

Zach couldn't sleep Friday night. He and Chris had each promised to be in bed by nine so that they'd be rested and ready for the game against the Scorpions Saturday morning. But Zach was too wound up with nervous energy to sleep.

He tried lying on his right side, then his left side. He curled his knees up to his stomach, then stretched his toes down to the foot of the bed. He pulled the blanket up to his chin, then fought off all the covers by madly pumping his legs. He tried getting up and drinking a glass of water, but that just made him get up again 15 minutes later to use the bathroom.

He was getting more and more frustrated, and that just made it more impossible to sleep.

Finally, when it was almost midnight, Zach laid back and stared at the ceiling. He remembered something his dad had taught him to do before football games.

It was called visualization, which was a fancy word that meant thinking about playing well. Not just to think about it, but to actually make a mental picture of doing it. To see himself running a pass route, faking out a Scorpion defender, and catching a touchdown pass from Chris. To see himself intercepting a pass and taking it all the way for a pick six.

It was hard for Zach to believe that such a fun and easy thing as daydreaming about being a great player could actually be helpful in a real game. But his dad had insisted that even pro players used visualization and it worked for them.

Even if it didn't help in tomorrow's game, it worked Friday night. Zach finally relaxed. And by the time he had watched himself score his seventh touchdown of the game, he was asleep.

-15-
Season Opener

"Where ya been?" Chris called out from mid-field as Zach hopped off his bike behind the end zone.

"How long you been here?" Zach asked as he trotted toward his best friend. Both boys were wearing their powder blue Lightning uniforms. Their blue helmets had white lightning bolts on both sides.

"Since seven thirty." Chris stood at the 50-yard line, spinning a ball between his large hands. "But I guess you care more about your beauty rest than getting ready for the game."

"Gimme a break, it's seven thirty-five!" Zach protested with a laugh.

"You owe me, dude. Five minutes is five minutes."

"Okay, fine. What's the price?"

"Thirty push-ups."

"Thirty push-ups! For five minutes?! How about five push-ups and five jumping jacks?"

"Make 'em Marine style for whining like a baby."

Zach knelt down on the grass and leaned forward, extending his right hand for support. "You're evil, you know that, Chris?"

Zach and Chris had made this deal when they were playing for the Zephyrs last year. If either of them were late to a game or a practice, the other got to decide the punishment.

Chris counted out loud as Zach began the one-handed push-ups. When he said, "Thirty!" Zach switched hands and pumped out ten more.

"Not bad for a string-bean wide receiver." Chris laughed as he held out a hand and pulled Zach to his feet. "Now, go deep!"

Zach didn't have time to catch his breath. He sprinted downfield, racing to grab Chris's high-arcing pass.

The two boys had the field to themselves for 45 minutes before the other players began arriving for the nine o'clock game. That's the way they planned it. Extra time to work on pass routes and speed drills. Visualization might be helpful, but Zach knew it couldn't replace old-fashioned hard work.

Coach Mac huddled with the Lightning defensive unit on the sideline before the game. The Scorpions had won the coin toss and elected to receive the kick-off.

"Owen, kick it away from number 14. He's their quarterback, and their fastest player. Ends and outside backers, don't let 14 get outside. Turn him inside when he's rolling out to pass. Everyone else pursue to the ball and drive through your tackles." Coach Mac held out his hand and the players all grabbed it.

"One-two-three!" Coach Mac's voice was powerful, even though he didn't speak any louder than usual.

The players all shouted, "Lightning!" They broke the huddle and raced onto the field.

The Scorpion eleven, wearing silver helmets and jerseys with black numbers, spread out to block for number 14. Dante Webb, their star player, waited for the kick-off at the 25-yard line.

Owen Carlson teed up the football. Five players were lined up on either side of him. Zach and Chris stood next to each other on the right flank.

"Ready to rock and roll, amigo?" Chris grinned at Zach.

Zach nodded, barely able to hold back the surge of energy pumping through his body. He turned and saw his mom and Kate standing on the sideline, waving to him and shouting something he couldn't hear. For a moment, everything was strangely silent, even though it looked like everybody was yelling.

That's when Zach remembered his dad, far away in Connecticut instead of being here. He looked again at his mom and little sister.

He pictured his dad standing beside them, giving him a thumb's up. Visualization. Maybe it worked for things besides football. Like bringing his dad back home.

Zach was so completely focused on the vision of his father that he didn't see Owen race toward the tee and send the football into the sky.

Chris took two strides downfield, noticed Zach wasn't next to him, and turned to yell back. "Zach!"

Zach's head swiveled. The energy inside him suddenly broke free. He rocketed forward, catching and passing Chris within ten yards. He was a blur, a streak, like the lightning bolt on the side of his blue helmet.

47

Coach Mac groaned as Owen's kick-off sailed end over end straight to Dante Webb, the player Owen was supposed to kick the ball away from. Dante caught the ball at the 30, took one step to the left, and Zach flattened him.

The other Lightning defenders roared their approval as Chris and Zach jumped at each other in a chest bump.

"Dude, that was awesome!" Chris shouted.

Zach was still enjoying the celebration as he moved to his free safety position. But the Scorpions weren't huddling up. They were already at the line of scrimmage and ready to snap the ball.

Dylan Yeager, the Lightning defensive captain, frantically called out the signals. "Cover three! Cover three!"

Before Zach could move into position, Dante Webb was dropping back to pass. Out of the corner of his eye, Zach could see a Scorpion wide-out flash by cornerback William Chen.

Normally, he would have matched that wide-out stride for stride. But Zach hadn't been ready for the snap of the ball and now it was too late to get into coverage. All he could do was watch helplessly as the ball sailed through the air into the wide-out's hands!

Zach gave chase and closed the gap. He dove, but grabbed nothing but air. Zach skidded face first across the goal line as the Scorpion wide-out cruised into the end zone for six points.

Zach turned with a mouthful of grass as he faced his stunned teammates.

"My fault, guys," Zach muttered miserably.

"Forget it, Fargo." Dylan slapped Zach's shoulder pads. "We'll get it back."

The Scorpions quickly lined up for the extra-point attempt without huddling. As the Lightning scrambled into position, Dante Webb ran a quarterback draw into the end zone for the two-point conversion.

Zach's head was down as he followed the other Lightning defenders to the sideline where Coach Mac was waiting with hands on hips. But two huge Scorpion linemen suddenly blocked Zach's path.

He looked up to see Max and Dalton Schwartz – the twins who had tried to make Zach's life miserable during their season together in the peewees.

"Nice play, diaper baby!" sneered Max.

"Yeah, thanks for the six points!" Dalton laughed.

They both looked to see if any officials were watching, then shoved Zach to the ground. As they lumbered away, a gob of spit landed next to Zach's feet. He sat there in disbelief.

How could his first game in the youth majors have started so terribly? Less than one minute had passed and he had already given up a touchdown and been dumped on his butt by the two people he hated more than anyone on the planet.

When Zach reached the sideline huddle he expected to be chewed out by Coach Mac. He knew he deserved it, putting his team in an 8-0 hole. To his surprise, Coach Mac didn't seem angry at all.

"It's my fault, boys. I didn't prepare you for their no-huddle offense." He looked at Zach and smiled. "I see you have some friends on the Scorpions, Zach."

"They're a couple of idiots," Chris snarled.

"Forget about them. The rest of the ballgame starts right now." Coach Mac held out his hand for the team to grab. "One-two-three!"

"Lightning!" the players shouted louder than ever.

Thanks to Chris, the Lightning tied the score on their first possession. He hit Zach on two straight down-and-out patterns to get the ball into Scorpion territory.

Then Chris scrambled out of the pocket, broke two tackles, and outran the Scorpion secondary to score from 47 yards.

The Lightning added a two-point conversion when Chris ran the option and made a perfect pitch to Jared Greenberg, who strolled into the end zone untouched.

The score remained tied 8-8 at halftime as both teams' defenses made big plays to end drives. Chris hit Connor Shaw on a crossing pattern deep in Scorpion territory, but Connor dropped the ball and a Scorpion defender fell on it.

Then, with only seconds left in the first half, Dante Webb broke free on a quarterback bootleg. He raced down the sideline, headed for what seemed to be a sure touchdown.

Zach tried to angle toward him, but knew he couldn't get there in time. Fortunately, Chris appeared out of nowhere, blowing past Zach.

He dove for Dante's ankles, caught his back foot and brought him down at the five-yard line as time ran out in the first half.

It hadn't taken Zach, Chris, and the other first-year Lightning players long to realize that the Schwartz twins weren't the only dirty players on the Scorpions. Whenever they thought they could get away with it, the Scorpions tripped, kicked, and punched their opponents.

Apparently, their coach and the parents on their sideline thought that style of play was just fine because all they did was cheer whenever a Scorpion player sucker-punched one of the Lightning boys.

Coach Mac saw the anger and frustration building in his young players, so he used the half-time to talk about it.

"That's their game, boys. That's the only way the Scorpions think they can win. But it's not our game. If we stick to how we play the game, we can win. If we play their way, then the game is theirs."

It seemed simple the way Coach Mac said it, but he knew he was asking a lot of the boys on his team. He knew it wasn't easy for them to ignore the dirty plays. He knew how hard it could be for

52

anyone, an adult or a young football player, to maintain focus while being constantly attacked.

That's what made Coach Mac a great coach and an even greater man. He expected a lot from his team because he knew that was the only way they would achieve greatness.

But greatness isn't usually reached in one try. It wasn't reached by the Lightning in this first football game of the season.

Chris scored on another long touchdown run to start the third quarter. But Dante Webb returned the next kickoff all the way to tie the score.

Midway through the third quarter, Jared Greenberg caught Chris's shovel pass and took it to the house. Chris bulled his way into the end zone for the two-point conversion to give the Lightning a 24-16 lead.

On the next Scorpion drive, Zach's nightmare returned when he cut in front of the wide-out and leaped to make an interception. But he misjudged the strength of the Scorpion quarterback's arm.

Dante Webb's pass whizzed past Zach's fingers and into the arms of the Scorpion wide-out who was standing in the end zone.

The Scorpions quickly lined up for the extra-point attempt, only a two-point conversion away from tying the score at 24. Dante Webb took the snap, dropped back, then lowered his shoulder and dashed forward on another quarterback draw.

But this time Zach recognized the play and shot forward from his safety position. He drove his shoulder pads into the quarterback's chest, knocking him backwards onto the ground short of the goal line. The Lightning kept their 24-22 lead!

After both teams were forced to punt in the fourth quarter, the Lightning began a final march down the field. All they had to do was run out the clock to win the game.

On an important fourth down play from their 40-yard line, Chris ran a sweep around right end. Zach leveled the Scorpion outside linebacker to clear a path for Chris.

Chris neared the first down marker, cut inside, and was tackled by Dalton Schwartz. Before getting up, Dalton dug his fist into Chris's ribs. Chris pushed him off.

As the two were standing eye to eye, Dalton spit at him. Chris exploded, knocking Dalton back to the ground and jumping on him.

The officials' whistles blew and their yellow penalty flags flew in the air. Zach was the first one to try to stop the fight. As he struggled to pull Chris away, Dalton swung his cleat and kicked the back of Zach's leg.

The officials had only seen Chris jump on Dalton. They had missed what Dalton had done to start it. The head ref signaled a 15-yard penalty against the Lightning for unsportsmanlike conduct.

"He spit in my face!" Chris protested.

The ref glared at Chris and pointed to the side-line. "You're out of the game!"

Chris bucked free from Zach's grasp, but Dylan Yeager wrapped his thick arms around the young quarterback in a bear hug, making sure he didn't do anything else to make the situation worse for his team.

As Chris trudged off the field, Zach watched Max and the other Scorpions laughing as they gave Dalton high fives.

Facing fourth down and 17, the Lightning were forced to punt. Although the Scorpions had only two minutes to score, Chris was no longer on the field at middle linebacker. Coach Mac put in Owen

Carlson to play Chris's position, but Owen was clueless.

Seeing this advantage, Dante Webb led the Scorpions on a drive down the field. They gained at least eight or ten yards each time they attacked the middle of the Lightning defense.

The safeties, Zach and Marcus, moved up closer to the line of scrimmage to help plug up the hold created by Chris's absence. But that was risky because the Scorpions might throw deep.

The ball was on the Lightning 20 with half a minute to play. As Zach feared, he saw the Scorpion wide-out flash past him on a deep route. The ball left the quarterback's hand and sailed high in the air.

Zach turned and raced back. The ball was going over his reach toward the receiver in the end zone. Zach leaped and felt the ball graze the tip of his finger.

The ball bounced off the wide-out's hands and fell incomplete! Zach wasn't sure if he had deflected the ball or not, but it didn't matter.

There was only enough time for one more play. One more stop and the Lightning would win!

Dylan barked out the defensive coverage. "Prevent! Prevent!"

Zach and the other three defensive backs stood on the goal line, willing to give up anything except a touchdown.

But instead of lining up in their usual shotgun formation, the Scorpions lined up for a field goal attempt. Before the Lightning could change their positions, the ball was snapped and Dante Webb booted the ball high in the air.

Zach turned and looked up. His heart sank as the ball split the uprights. The Scorpions won the game 25-24!

As the Scorpions mobbed their star player, the stunned Lightning defenders trudged off the field. As devastated as they all felt, no one felt worse than Chris. He buried his face in his hands, his shoulders heaving up and down with each sob.

Coach Mac's expression didn't change even though he had just seen his team let a certain victory slip away. He gathered the boys together on the sideline, then turned to Chris who was still slumped over on a bench.

"Chris. We need you."

Chris looked up, his eyes red. He joined the huddle, but stared down at his feet. Zach put his hand on Chris's shoulder.

Coach Mac's voice was strong and steady. "You boys gave everything you had out there today. I'm proud of you." He looked over at Chris. "All of you."

Chris nodded, still unable to force his eyes up to the others.

Coach Mac held out his hand. "One-two-three!"

The boys' voices were louder than ever. "Lightning!"

-16-
Learning from a Loss

"I don't want to hear anybody trying to take the blame for the loss on Saturday." Those were Coach Mac's first words at Tuesday's practice.

Every player on the Lightning thought Coach Mac was speaking directly to him. Each boy had been replaying the game in his mind, over and over, remembering every mistake that contributed to the loss.

Connor Shaw remembered his fumble deep in Scorpion territory. Dylan Yeager remembered the missed tackles when he almost sacked the Scorpion quarterback. Jared Greenberg remembered the pass he dropped in the fourth quarter. Luis Chavez remembered the two offside penalties he caused. William Chen remembered being beaten on a post pattern by the Scorpion wide-out. Owen Carlson remembered being unable to do anything to stop the final Scorpion drive.

Zach, of course, couldn't stop thinking about the long touchdown pass he gave up on the game's first play. If he had just reacted sooner. He should have seen the wide-out's move and chosen a better angle to the ball.

That was exactly the kind of pass play he loved to defend. Let the wide-out's eyes grow big as the ball sails toward his waiting hands, then swoop in at the last moment, snatch the ball out of the air and head back up field with the interception.

No one, though, felt worse than Chris. He hadn't been able to sleep or even eat much since the game. He felt so stupid for falling for Dalton's trick and losing his temper. He knew the Lightning would've won if he'd been on the field those final two minutes.

The first night Chris cried for hours. He hadn't done that in years. Not since the day his dad had left.

"We're a team. Remember that, boys. No one takes the credit for a win and no one takes the blame for a loss. We win as a team and, if we lose, we lose as a team."

Coach Mac didn't say another word about the contest against the Scorpions. His focus at practice was squarely on preparations for the next game against the Eagles. Even though the Eagles had finished in last place each of the past two seasons, Coach Mac acted like they were world champs.

During the game against the Scorpions, Coach Mac had filled his playbook with notes about what he saw on the field. While most coaches were arguing with the refs and shouting instructions to their players, Coach Mac was busy writing. He used those notes to pinpoint to his players what they needed to do to improve their performance.

"When you're pass blocking, Luis, you want to use your feet to stay between the rusher and your QB."

"Got it, Coach," Luis nodded. "I won't make that mistake again."

"It's not a mistake, son." He turned for all the players to hear. "You boys didn't make any mistakes last Saturday. You just need more time to learn how to play football. That's what the season is for."

Coach Mac knew how to make everything seem positive. Mistakes weren't really mistakes. They were actually good things because they showed you what you needed to practice and learn.

By the end of Tuesday's practice, the boys on the Lightning all felt a lot better about themselves. Chris, most of all.

-17-
Blow-out

The Eagles had finished in last place two years in a row for a simple reason. They weren't very good. Their quarterback couldn't throw a spiral. Their defense didn't know how to tackle. And their punter usually kicked the ball straight up in the air, then had to dodge out of the way so it wouldn't land on his helmet.

But the Eagles' biggest problem was their coach. He spent the entire game screaming at his players. And when he wasn't yelling, he was busy flirting with all the moms on the sideline.

It was embarrassing. The Eagle players all acted like they couldn't wait for the game to end so they could go do something they actually liked.

The Lightning players, on the other hand, were having so much fun they wished the game could've lasted another couple of quarters. Jared Greenberg returned the opening kickoff for a touchdown. And it only got better from there!

Chris and Zach connected on three touchdown passes. Dylan Yeager had half a dozen sacks. William Chen picked off a pass and ran it back for a score. And Owen Carlson kicked five straight extra-points. That was just the first half. The score was 35-0.

Those sad Eagles had to be given a lot of credit for showing up for the second half. Coach Mac must have felt sorry for them. He called a bunch of running plays to eat up the clock and hold the score down.

Even so, Jared and Chris each dashed for touchdowns. Owen booted a 38-yard field goal. And Lucas Higney grabbed a punt out of the air just as it was about to hit the Eagle punter on the head. Lucas pranced into the end zone, waving the ball for everyone to see. Then he did a ridiculous chicken dance and took a deep bow.

The final score was 59-0.

All the parents behind the Lightning bench cheered like crazy and congratulated the team for their spectacular performance. The boys high-fived and chest bumped each other when the game finally ended.

Only one person on the Lightning sideline wasn't acting all happy. Coach Mac didn't like the way Lucas had celebrated that last touchdown. He pulled Lucas aside for a private conversation.

"It's fine to feel good when you make a play like that. But there's no need to make the other team feel even worse than they already do. That kind of showing off has no place on the football field, son. Or anywhere else on this earth."

"Yes, sir." Lucas' voice sounded small, like the way he felt.

Coach Mac called the boys over for the post-game huddle.

"You boys gave everything you had out there today. I'm proud of you." It was the same thing Coach Mac had said after the Scorpions game. And he didn't sound excited.

Zach couldn't believe it. He looked over at Chris. Chris was just as surprised that their coach didn't seem thrilled by the 59 point victory.

Coach Mac held out his hand. "One-two-three!"

"Lightning!"

As the huddle broke, Zach couldn't help himself. He had to ask Coach Mac how he really felt about the game.

"Coach, whaddya think? Pretty great game, huh?"

Coach Mac put a fatherly hand on Zach's shoulder. "You boys are learning how to play football." He tapped his playbook. "But there are a few more things to learn. That's what the season is for."

18

On a Roll

The Lightning continued their winning ways in the next three regular season games.

They pounded the Blitz 26-6 as Chris threw touchdown passes to four different receivers.

Jared Greenberg made a pair of long touchdown runs and Chris recovered a fumble and returned it for a score as the Lightning beat the Ambush 20-10.

The Rattlers fell to the Lightning 34-6. Zach got his first two interceptions of the season, returning one for six points. Unfortunately, Jared Greenberg injured his ankle late in the game.

Jared had taken a hand-off from Chris and sped around left end. As he planted his left foot to cut back, a Rattler linebacker hit him. Jared's body fell forward, but his left ankle twisted under the linebacker's heavy body.

Jared was a tough kid, but the pain brought tears to his eyes as he lay crumpled on the field. Kelvin's mom was a doctor and she rushed onto the field with Jared's parents. Doctor Jones had been volunteering all season as the Lightning's team doctor.

The doctor took one look at Jared's twisted ankle and placed her hand on his forehead to calm him.

"You're going to be fine, young man," she assured him. The doctor looked at Jared's parents. "We'll need to take him to the hospital for x-rays."

With his dad on one side of Jared and Coach Mac on the other, the injured running back hopped off the field on one foot. All the parents on both sidelines gave him a standing ovation.

The x-rays showed that Jared's ankle was broken. He would miss the rest of the season. It was a huge loss for the Lightning. Jared was the team's best runner and a hard-hitting cornerback.

At the next practice, Coach Mac announced that Curtis Briggs would be Jared's replacement. Curtis was the worst player on the team. He hadn't started a game all season, and had only subbed in when Coach Mac wanted to go easy on the other team.

"I'm gonna play?" Curtis' eyes were wide behind his thick black glasses.

He didn't know much about football, but everyone agreed that Curtis had more guts than

68

anyone on the team. He never once backed down when he was getting the snot knocked out of him at practice.

Maybe that would make up for his inexperience.

19

Shovel and Go

In the final game of the regular season, the Lightning had their most difficult test since the opening loss to the Scorpions. The Panthers had a so-so 3-2 record, but one of their wins had been a 12-7 victory over the Scorpions.

The Panther defense was the best in the league. They played low-scoring games, and would have had a better record if Rashard Thompson, their fast-as-lightning quarterback, hadn't been injured early in the season.

Fortunately for the Panthers, and unfortunately for the Lightning, Rashard was back in the line-up for this final contest. And he was determined to make up for all those games he'd missed.

On the Panthers' first possession, Rashard ran five straight times, dodging and darting through the Lightning defense for huge gains. On the sixth play, he started around right end, reversed direction when Dylan Yeager and Lucas Higney were about to grab him, and outran the Lightning defenders for a 20-yard touchdown. The Panther kicker booted the extra-point to make the score 7-0.

The Lightning offense took the field, but the Panther defense was like a brick wall. With Jared Greenberg on crutches on the sideline, the Lightning running attack fell on Chris's shoulders.

Normally, that wouldn't have been a problem because Chris was such a strong and swift runner. But every time Coach Mac called a quarterback rollout, the Panthers' defensive line would push past the blockers and swarm Chris before he could even escape the pocket.

It wasn't any better when they tried to pass. Zach ripped off precise pass patterns, practically breaking the ankles of the Panther defensive back. But each time, he turned back to see Chris buried under a pile of defensive sackers.

The game didn't turn into a rout because Coach Mac called a time-out after the first Panther touchdown. He announced a major defensive adjustment to try to stop Rashard.

"Chris, I want you to forget your normal assignments and stick with number one wherever he goes. Follow him every play until the play is over, even if he doesn't have the ball."

"Okay, Coach."

"Who's going to cover Chris's territory?" asked Dylan, the captain of the defense.

"Safeties, Zach and Marcus, pinch in. Outside backers, Lucas and Kelvin, do the same. Number one will have to beat us with his arm, not with his legs."

The strategy worked. Play after play, Chris hounded Rashard, flying into the Panther backfield at full-speed and tackling him for losses or forcing him into hurried throws.

But nothing the Lightning tried on offense worked against the tough Panther D. The score remained 7-0 into the fourth quarter.

No team wants to end their season with a loss. The last game of the season is the one that's remembered the most through all those long months until the next season begins.

But the Lightning had an even more important reason why they desperately wanted to win this final regular season game. If they beat the Panthers, the Lightning would finish with a 5-1 record and a first place tie with the Scorpions.

That meant the Lightning would play the Scorpions in the Mighty Bowl, the youth majors championship game!

If the Panthers won, they would be the team to face the Scorpions for the championship. The Lightning's season would be over.

The start of the fourth quarter looked promising for the Lightning, even though they were starting deep in their own territory at the eight yard line. In a defensive struggle like the game had been, most coaches would call a safe play like a run up the middle.

But Coach Mac signaled for a double reverse, a play they had practiced all year but had never run in a game. Chris took the snap and started to the left on a sweep. But he suddenly pitched the ball back to William Chen, who was running to the right.

As the Panther defense turned their pursuit toward William, he handed the ball off to Zach, who was speeding to the left ten yards behind the line of scrimmage in his own end zone.

The Panther right cornerback wasn't fooled. He came up fast and lowered his shoulder as Zach took the hand-off in the end zone. If he tackled

73

Zach for a safety, the Panthers would go up 9-0 and the Lightning would need two scores to avoid defeat.

The cornerback dove at Zach's knees. But Zach hurdled over him. He turned the corner and raced up the sideline.

For a moment it looked like Zach might take it all the way. Mrs. Fargo jumped up and down, screaming like a high school cheerleader. Kate tried to run alongside Zach, but was quickly left behind. Chris stood back on the ten yard line and yelled at Zach to go. Even Coach Mac dropped his playbook and waved his arms to urge Zach on.

The only player on the Panthers with a chance to catch Zach was Rashard Thompson. Rashard didn't head toward Zach as he sped with the ball up the sideline. Instead, Rashard angled farther down field, aiming for where Zach would be in a matter of seconds.

His plan worked. The two speedsters collided at the Panther ten yard line and Zach was knocked out of bounds.

Rashard had prevented the game-tying touchdown, but the Lightning now had their first real opportunity to put points on the board. As everyone hustled downfield for the next play, the Panther coach called a time-out. He could see that his defense needed to regroup after Zach's 82-yard run.

On first and goal from the ten, Chris ran a quarterback draw through a huge hole thanks to crushing blocks by Dylan Yeager and Parker Coates. Chris was finally brought down at the Panther three. Chris bulled his way forward on second down and was tackled one yard short of the goal line.

Third and one. The Lightning had two chances to gain one yard and even the score. Or even take the lead with a two-point conversion.

The players in the Lightning huddle could feel the energy build as Chris called the next play – another run behind Dylan and Parker.

They took their positions at the line of scrimmage. Chris barked out the signals. At the snap, Dylan and Parker charged forward, leveling the Panther defenders. Zach blocked the cornerback, then turned to watch the touchdown.

But something went wrong. Owen's snap sailed over Chris's head and bounced back to the 20 yard line! Chris turned to chase after the ball, but a blitzing Panther linebacker flattened him. Another linebacker scooped up the ball, with no one between him and the Lightning end zone 80 yards away.

Zach was running before he even knew what he was doing. He jumped over Chris and the defender who had tackled him. But the linebacker with the ball was already lumbering across the 50 yard line.

It was only moments ago that Zach was the one running with the ball toward the end zone. Now he was the only one who could prevent the Panther linebacker from scoring a touchdown. A touchdown that would put the game out of reach!

Zach ran faster than he ever had in his life. The linebacker was at the 20, still ten yards ahead of him.

A picture of a cheetah in cleats flashed through Zach's brain. He sped even faster. As the linebacker crossed the five-yard line, Zach was close enough to dive and tackle him. But their momentum would carry them into the end zone for a touchdown. Zach had only one option.

He swung out his right arm and punched the ball from behind. The ball flew from the surprised linebacker's hand just as he was about to cross the goal line! It skidded across the end zone and out of bounds!

The referee signaled a touchback. The Lightning got the ball back at their own 20. Zach had miraculously saved the Lightning from certain defeat.

But they would need another miracle to pull out a victory and move on to the Mighty Bowl. The Lightning had to go 80 yards to score. And there were only four minutes left in the game.

Chris threw a perfect strike to Kelvin Jones on first down. But the normally sure-handed tight end turned to run before catching the football. The pass fell incomplete on the 35-yard line.

On second down Chris dropped back to pass again, but the fierce Panther rush forced him out of the pocket. He scrambled to his left, looked downfield and saw Zach breaking free at midfield.

Chris cocked his arm and, just as he was about to release the ball, a Panther defender hit his elbow. The ball sailed out of bounds.

Third and ten with under three minutes to play. Coach Mac signaled a comeback pass to Zach. It was a low-risk play that would gain ten yards, but wouldn't take much time off the clock.

As Chris took the snap, Zach ran straight downfield 12 yards, then turned back for the ball. Normally, the ball would arrive just as he turned around. It was automatic. He and Chris had worked on the timing of this pass a million times.

But they had never practiced it against a defense as tough as this Panther unit. Chris had a blitzing linebacker in his face as he threw the pass. The ball hit Zach's shoulder pad just as he started his turn. The pass was incomplete.

Now the Lightning faced fourth down and ten at their own 20. They couldn't punt. There wasn't enough time left to get the ball back. They'd have to go for it. If they didn't pick up the first down, the game was basically over.

Chris looked to the sideline for the signal from Coach Mac, then relayed it to his teammates in the huddle.

"Right Shovel and Go on two." Chris's voice was surprisingly calm considering what a risky play he had just called.

Right Shovel and Go was a comeback pass like the one they'd just attempted. Except with a big twist. Zach had to sell the cornerback on a deep route, stop on a dime, turn and catch the pass, then make a lateral with the cornerback hitting him in the back. The Shovel and Go required perfect timing or it could backfire and end in an interception or fumble.

The Lightning had worked on the play many times in practice, but had never tried it in a game. And in practice, Jared Greenberg had been the running back who sped by and grabbed the pitch from Zach.

With Jared out of the line-up, that job belonged to Curtis. And they had never practiced it with Curtis.

Nobody moved in the huddle. Everyone just stared straight ahead. They were all thinking the same thing. The Shovel and Go was risky even with Jared running it. With Curtis, it seemed hopeless.

Curtis gulped hard, eyes big behind thick glasses. Chris looked around at the worried faces in the huddle. The team needed someone to lead them through this desperate situation.

Chris didn't realize it, but he had changed in the weeks since losing his temper on the field and being kicked out of the season opener against the Scorpions. He had learned a lot more than football from Coach Mac. He had learned how to be a leader.

"We're going to win this game, men." Chris's voice was calm and confident.

His teammates all studied his face, as if to be sure he was for real.

Chris slowly grinned, "Piece of cake."

Everyone suddenly relaxed, grinning back and feeling their confidence soar. Even Curtis looked less terrified.

Chris held out his right hand. "One-Two-Three!"

The other players grasped Chris's hand, shouting "Lightning!"

They Lightning broke the huddle and charged up to the line of scrimmage. Chris surveyed the Panther defense as he barked out fake signals.

"Red, 42, Bulldog, hut, hut!"

Owen snapped the ball. Zach ran five steps and suddenly turned while the cornerback continued to backpedal. Chris pump-faked left, freezing the blitzing linebacker, then pivoted and threw a laser at Zach.

The pass hit Zach's shoulder pads and bounced. Zach reached up and snared the ball with his fingertips. The cornerback charged forward to deliver a hit and try to jar the ball loose.

Zach saw a blur streaking to his left. It was Curtis. Zach swung the ball down, then shoveled it just ahead of the blur.

The cornerback exploded into Zach's back. Curtis reached out for the lateral, juggling the ball between his hands as he ran.

Curtis crossed the 30, passing the first down marker. There wasn't a Panther within 20 yards of him! Rashard Thompson had bought Chris's pump fake and was taken out of the play.

The other Lightning players jumped up and down, yelling their heads off as they watched Curtis race untouched into the end zone. The score was 7-6. An extra-point would tie it. And Owen hadn't missed an extra-point kick all season.

But Coach Mac had other plans. As his players mobbed Curtis in the end zone, he was flipping through his playbook for the perfect two-point conversion. He found what he was looking for, then sent the signal to Chris.

As the Lightning lined up for the play that would determine the winner of the game, Zach could see that the Panther defense looked like they had already lost. The Shovel and Go touchdown had shaken them badly.

Chris took the snap, jumped up and threw a perfect lob pass to Kelvin in the end zone. Kelvin simply reached up for the ball like a power forward grabbing a rebound. The only players who tackled him were his teammates who jumped on him in celebration.

The Panthers had time for a Hail Mary, but Zach batted Rashard Thompson's pass to the ground and the game was over. The Lightning won 8-7!

The regular season was over, but Coach Mac's team had one more football game to play – against the Scorpions in the Mighty Bowl!

-20-
Missing Dad and Missing Practice

Even though Zach's dad was a thousand miles away in Connecticut, his daily texts, emails, and phone calls made it seem almost like he was still with the family. He and his wife discussed bills and vacation plans just like they always did.

Kate uploaded her math homework so her dad could tutor her at night. And Zach eagerly gave his father a play-by-play account of each game and practice.

Of course, it wasn't the same as having his dad there watching Zach play and giving him all those thumbs-up. Each time Zach hung up the phone, he felt an emptiness inside. His mom knew Zach would need extra hugs just to get him to eat his dinner.

His dad missing the entire regular season had been tough on both of them. The thought of Mr. Fargo not being there to see Zach in the Mighty Bowl was more than either of them could handle.

Fortunately, Zach's dad had a partial solution. He told Zach about it when they talked Monday night.

"Please, Dad!" Zach had tried his best to be strong the past six weeks, but now he couldn't help himself. "Can't you come back just for the weekend?"

"I wish I could, son. But you know the deal. I promised I'd be back by Thanksgiving. That's only three more weeks."

"But, Dad, it's the Mighty Bowl!"

"Believe me, Zach. I want to see that game more than anything. And I figured out a way I can do it!"

"Huh? What do you mean, Dad?"

"The satellite company heard about the game. Actually, we've been watching all the games Mom recorded. Some of the guys got together and figured out a way to send a camera crew to the game. I'll be watching it live!"

"The Mighty Bowl's gonna be televised?!"

"That's the plan."

"That's great, Dad! I'll be sure to wave at you!"

Zach couldn't wait to tell everyone the news at practice the next day. He planned to tell Chris on the way to school that morning.

But Chris didn't appear on his bike at their usual meeting place and he was absent from school that day.

All the Lightning players were amazed to hear that their game against the Scorpions was going to be on TV. Even if it was only shown in Connecticut.

"Are you for real?" Kelvin and a few others were still having a hard time believing it was true.

"My dad set it all up!"

"Yeah!" Parker nodded. "Zach's dad works for a satellite company!"

Zach grinned proudly. "It's gonna be the best Mighty Bowl ever!"

As everyone cheered, Coach Mac did a quick head count. "Where's Chris?"

The players all looked at each other, shrugging their shoulders.

"He wasn't at school today," Zach responded. "He must be sick or something."

"First I've heard of it," Coach Mac grumbled. "Alright, boys, pair off for footwork drills."

Most of the players had missed a practice or two because of dental appointments or illness. Coach Mac knew those kinds of things happened.

He had a simple rule for it. You were excused from practice if you let him know ahead of time.

The only exception was if there was a family emergency or you got run over by a truck on your way to practice and were in the hospital. Then your parents were supposed to let him know what the deal was and Coach Mac would say it was okay.

If you missed practice and you didn't let him know ahead of time, or if you weren't in the hospital, the penalty was you couldn't play in that week's game.

Lucas Higney was the only boy who had broken that rule. He had to sit out the Ambush game because he skipped practice to go see the latest Centipedeman movie. Lucas was miserable as he watched the game from the sideline. He said the Centipedeman movie wasn't even that good.

All practice, Zach kept wondering about Chris. He figured Chris must be real sick to miss practice, especially the week of the Mighty Bowl.

And his mom must be sick, too. Or else she would've called Coach Mac to explain everything.

Anyway, Zach thought, she'll probably get a hold of Coach Mac tomorrow and explain everything and it'll all be okay.

But Chris's mom didn't get ahold of Coach Mac the next day. She didn't get ahold of him at all that whole week.

-21-
Losing a Friend

After practice Zach decided to ride out to Chris's house to see how he was doing. Chris was his best friend, and Zach was worried about him. Not to mention there was no way the Lightning could win the Mighty Bowl without Chris in the lineup.

The rusty white minivan was gone, and when Zach walked up the sagging wooden steps, he could see that the glass in the front door was broken out. Zach peered in through the broken glass.

"Hello?" he called. In the dimness, Zach could see that the tiny house was empty and that the refrigerator door was left open.

The next day before school, Zach found Chris locking up his bike at the bike rack.

"You guys move?"

Chris answered without looking up. "Yep."

"Is that why you missed practice?"

"Yep."

Chris brushed past Zach and headed for the front door. Zach followed him.

"Did you tell Coach Mac? He'll excuse you."

Chris suddenly pivoted to face Zach.

"Look, can we stop talking about this? We moved, end of story."

As Chris went into the school, Zach angrily called out after him. "I thought we were friends! Friends are supposed to talk to each other!"

It made no sense to Zach why Chris acted so angry. People moved to new houses all the time. What was the big deal? You'd think he'd be happy to move out of that depressing house. And why didn't Chris tell Coach Mac that he had to help his mom with the moving?

Zach and Chris didn't speak to each other the rest of the day. That was okay at first. Zach was mad and didn't care if Chris ever talked to him for as long as they lived.

But when he woke up Thursday morning, Zach was real grumpy and didn't know why.

He had no interest in the new sports magazine his mom had left on the breakfast table. He snapped at Kate when she asked him to please pass the cereal box.

He even shouted, "Leave me alone!" when his mom reminded him to put his football equipment in the car because she was taking him to practice right after his after-school science club.

Zach's mom sensed what was troubling him. He was lying on his bed, staring at the ceiling, when she poked her head in to tell him it was time to leave for school.

"Westridge High's homecoming game is tomorrow night, Zach. Want to ask Chris to come?"

Zach immediately wished Chris would say yes and they'd have a great time like always. They would bring the mini football and toss it back and forth behind the end zone like real high school players.

"I don't think he'd want to go," Zach said softly and turned over, burying his face in the pillow.

-22-
A New Quarterback

Zach and Chris didn't speak to each other at school that day either. Zach desperately wanted to ask Chris if he'd talked to Coach Mac about missing practice on Tuesday. But he figured that would get all cleared up at this afternoon's practice.

But it didn't get cleared up. Chris didn't show up for practice again. And it was obvious from Coach Mac's first words that Chris was not going to be playing for the Lightning in the Mighty Bowl.

"We're making some line-up changes for the game on Saturday. Lucas, you'll be playing right wide-out."

Zach's eyes widened. Right wide-out! That was Zach's position! What had he done wrong to lose his starting spot?!

"Owen starts at middle linebacker."

Middle linebacker was Chris's position! All the Lightning players knew what that meant. Their most valuable player definitely wasn't playing in the Mighty Bowl!

"Curtis again takes Jared's spot on both sides of the ball."

Jared winced at the news, even though the cast on his left foot wasn't coming off for three more weeks.

"Yes, sir!" Curtis looked at all his teammates and pumped his fist. He had grown up in the game against the Panthers.

"And playing quarterback…"

Zach and the other boys waited expectantly to hear who would be taking Chris's place as QB. Zach couldn't think of anyone on the team who could play that position without totally embarrassing himself and ruining any chance the Lightning had for victory.

"Zach," Coach Mac ended his announcement.

Zach didn't quite understand what Coach Mac had just said. "What, Coach?"

"You're starting at QB."

"Me? But, Coach, I can't play quarterback!"

"You did in the peewees."

"Only till Chris joined the team! I was awful! Right, Parker? Right, Austin?"

Zach looked at his former Zephyr teammates to back him up. But they were too stunned by the thought of Chris not playing to speak.

"I can't throw like Chris!"

Coach Mac had already made up his mind. "You can run. We'll be calling a lot of running plays."

No one spoke or even moved. Their hopes of a glorious Mighty Bowl victory had suddenly disappeared. They now all wished that the game wasn't going to be televised. They didn't want anyone to see the Lightning get crushed by the Scorpions.

"You're our only option, Zach." Coach Mac tapped his playbook. "And I have a couple tricks in here that are going to at least make the game interesting."

Coach Mac blew his whistle. The boys always jumped into action when they heard that whistle. But this time it was all they could do to slowly drag themselves onto the practice field.

The entire practice was devoted to working with the offense. Lucas did his best to learn the wide receiver routes, but he kept confusing slant and fade patterns. Coach Mac told him not to worry about it because they weren't going to be throwing many passes.

Zach at least had a basic understanding of the quarterback position. He had mostly run the ball during the short time he quarterbacked the Zephyrs offense. So he knew how to hand off, roll out on sweeps, and follow his blockers. And he knew exactly where the receivers were supposed to run, even if they didn't always know.

Most important of all, the hours he'd spent practicing with Chris made Zach realize how a quarterback's job differed from all the other players on offense.

Position players only had to know their role and the small part of the field they played on. The quarterback had to see the whole field and all the players on it. They had to react to everything at once. It was an extremely difficult thing to do. And only the best quarterbacks could do it well.

Over and over, Coach Mac had the offense practice hand-offs, fake hand-offs, sweeps, quick pitches, laterals, and reverses. Zach fumbled the first two times he tried to hand-off to Curtis. He threw a pitch five yards behind William. And his lob pass sailed ten feet over Kelvin's outstretched arms.

But as the practice wore on, the hand-offs and reverses started clicking. Coach Mac mixed in a few short passes that Zach completed to Connor and Curtis.

Practice usually ended at 5:30 sharp. Parents were lined up in their cars waiting to pick up their sons when Coach Mac finally blew his whistle at 6:00. But instead of sending the boys off, he opened his playbook.

"Alright, boys, now we're going to run the Double Flea Flicker With Extra Sprinkles." Coach Mac had a twinkle in his eye as he said it.

The weary players couldn't help but be curious about what he wanted to show them.

Forty minutes later, they raced off the practice field excitedly. Their hopes for a victory in the Mighty Bowl had returned.

23

Homeless

Zach and his mom stopped at Lucky's Market on the way home from practice. Zach hated shopping, but that was one of the ways he tried to help out while his dad was gone.

"Oh, darn! I left the coupons in the car. Would you mind running out to get them, Zach?"

Zach was about to open the car door when he looked up and spotted Chris striding across the parking lot. Zach wanted to call to him, but watched silently as Chris unlocked his bike from the rack next to the store and rode away.

Zach looked back in the direction Chris had come from and saw the rusted white minivan with the black door parked in the far corner of the lot.

Zach forgot the coupons and walked over to the white minivan. No one was sitting in the front seats. Zach looked in the side window and his eyes grew big.

It looked like somebody was living in the van! Boxes of clothing, fast food wrappers, and two sleeping bags filled the van. Could it be that Chris and his mom…

Zach backed away, then ran as fast as he could back into the store. He found his mom examining grapefruit in the produce section.

"Mom!"

"Did you get the coupons?"

"No, Mom! Chris's homeless!"

It was true. Chris and his mom had been evicted because the owner of the house they had been renting wanted to tear it down and use the space to store old boats that nobody wanted.

He had missed the first football practice to help his mom move their furniture into a storage unit out by the interstate. He didn't go to the second practice because he was too angry and embarrassed to face the other boys.

Since then, they had been parking in different lots around town, hoping no one would notice they were living in the van.

"Hmm, I think you're right," Mrs. Fargo said as she peered in through the front window of the minivan. "It does look like they're living in here."

"Let's have them move into our house! Chris can have my bed and I'll sleep in my sleeping bag on the floor! And Chris's mom can sleep in the spare bedroom!"

"That's a wonderful idea, Zach. But it might not be that simple."

"Why not?"

"Well, they might not be comfortable with the whole situation."

"You think they're comfortable living here?! We gotta do something, Mom!"

"We will, Zach. Why don't we call your father and see what he thinks?"

When they called Zach's dad that night, he had a better idea.

"A guy I used to work with has a trailer sitting empty in the trailer park on the other side of Mapleton Street. It's small, but clean, and the rent would be cheap."

Zach had liked the idea of he and Chris sharing a room. But he had to admit, his dad's idea sounded good.

24

Last Minute Call

When school was out Friday afternoon, Zach's mom was parked out front waiting for him. She was driving her husband's pick-up. A bunch of furniture was loaded in back.

"What's all that stuff for?" Zach asked as he slid onto the passenger seat.

"It belongs to the Riveras."

Zach gave his mom a puzzled look. She smiled and stepped on the gas pedal.

"Want to help them move into their new home?"

While Zach had been at school, his mom waited in Lucky's parking lot. When Chris's mom returned to the white minivan carrying a pile of laundry, Mrs. Fargo invited her to have a cup of coffee. That's when Mrs. Rivera tearfully shared the story of their unexpected homelessness.

Chris's father had left them when Chris was six. And now he stopped paying child support. That's why they'd been living in that run-down shack. Mrs. Rivera was going to school at night and working as a waitress all day. But she was having a hard time paying the bills.

Zach's mom listened, her eyes wet with tears. That's when she suggested her husband's idea about the trailer. Mrs. Rivera agreed that it sounded like a perfect solution.

"I don't know how we can thank you," she said as she wiped her eyes.

Mrs. Fargo reached out and squeezed Mrs. Rivera's hand. "You don't have to."

Before she picked up Zach, Mrs. Fargo had loaded the truck with the Rivera's belongings from the storage unit by the highway.

The rest of the afternoon, both moms and Kate filled the kitchen with dishes, pots and pans, and seasonings. The boys laughed and shouted happily as they carried the heavy furniture into the trailer.

Chris was excited to have a real home again. Zach was glad to help. And both boys were happy to have their best friend back again.

It was almost dark when they finished moving everything in. The five of them sat in a circle on the living room floor, eating pizza from a take-out box.

"We are so grateful for friends like you," Mrs. Rivera said to the Fargo family. "Right, Chris?"

"Definitely! Zach, did you see the beat-up half-pipe by the alley?"

"Yeah! I'll ride my bike over first thing tomorrow and we can try it out!"

"No, you won't!" Kate interrupted.

Everyone looked at Kate, waiting for her to explain.

"The Mighty Bowl's tomorrow!"

Zach looked at Chris and both their hearts sunk. Everything was perfect except one thing. One gigantic horrible thing! Chris wasn't allowed to play in the biggest game of their lives!

"Maybe it's not too late," Zach offered. "Maybe Coach Mac would let you play if he knew what happened."

"Yeah," Chris stared at the floor. He sounded like he didn't really believe it.

"That reminds me," Mrs. Rivera looked at Zach's mom and winked. "Coach Mac called earlier, Chris. He asked me to have you call him."

Chris's head jerked up. He looked from his mom to Zach, then back at his mom. "What did he want?"

"Why don't you call him and find out?"

Chris stared at his mom, fearful that he was feeling excited for nothing.

"Go call him!" Zach shouted, jumping to his feet and pulling Chris up with him. "Maybe he changed his mind!"

It was true. After having coffee earlier that day, Mrs. Fargo urged Chris's mom to call Coach Mac and explain what happened.

Coach Mac was totally sympathetic. He said it was a family emergency and excused Chris from Tuesday's practice since Chris was helping his mom move.

Coach Mac even stopped by the trailer around noon to check the electrical and water connections and make sure that everything was A-OK.

That's when he told Mrs. Rivera that he'd thought it over and it sounded like the missed practice on Thursday was a case of Chris being angry or humiliated or both.

He had decided that if Chris wanted to play in the Mighty Bowl, the youngster would have to make up for it by doing some community service first.

Chris's hand was shaking as he held the phone to his ear.

"Uh, hello? Coach Mac? This is Chris Rivera."

"Hello, Chris. Thank you for calling." Coach Mac's voice was as calm as always. He didn't sound mad at all.

Coach Mac told Chris how he knew all about what had happened. He said Chris was excused for missing Tuesday's practice because he was helping his mom move their stuff.

Chris breathed a sigh of relief. But Coach Mac wasn't finished.

"I know you've had a tough week, Chris. Life is filled with tough weeks. Now, about missing Thursday's practice."

Chris gulped hard.

"I can understand you were probably a whole mix of things – angry, sad, maybe embarrassed. Am I right, son?"

"Yeah," Chris whispered weakly.

"The fact is, Chris, having those kinds of feelings doesn't give us the right to let others down. Others who depend on us. From what I hear, that's what your father did to you and your mom.

103

That's *not* what I expect from a fine young man like you."

"Yes, sir."

"Do you still want to play in the Mighty Bowl?"

"Yes, sir!"

"Alright. First, you'll need to take responsibility for your actions. You let your team down yesterday."

"Yes, sir! I will!"

"Good. I want you to spend tomorrow morning picking up every piece of litter between the trailer park and the football field."

"Yes, sir! I'll do it, sir! I'll make Westridge look cleaner than it's ever looked!"

When both moms heard Chris's joyful whoop from the kitchen, they knew he'd just heard the best news of his life!

And when they saw Zach and Chris race out the door with a football, they knew last-minute preparations for the Mighty Bowl had begun!

-25-
Bobblehead Miracle

Zach knew he wouldn't be able to sleep that night, so he didn't even try. He sat in bed with his three-ring binder, thinking up new plays.

One of them he named "Satellite Switch". He chose that name because his dad worked for a satellite company and because the quarterback switched places with the wide receiver.

Zach ran the play over and over in his head, working out every tiny detail. His eyes started to droop and the pencil fell from his fingers to the floor.

The stadium was packed with 80,000 screaming football fanatics. A dozen television cameras caught the action from every possible angle. The ten-foot-tall Mighty Bowl trophy was wheeled out of a stadium tunnel by a team of security men.

The scoreboard clock ticked down... 20, 19, 18, 17... The score was Scorpions 35, Lightning 34.

The Scorpion defense dug in for one final stop as the Lightning offense hurried to the line of scrimmage. The ball was on the Lightning two-yard line. It was fourth down and forever.

12... 11... 10... 9... Zach, at quarterback, called out the signals. Chris moved in motion as the wide receiver.

Except that it was bobblehead Chris and bobblehead Zach! All of the players were bobbleheads! Even Coach Mac, standing on the sideline with his playbook, was a bobblehead!

5... 4... 3... 2...

The ball was snapped. Zach looked left, then right. His wooden head jiggled as he stared downfield.

Chris's bobblehead stretched back farther and farther as he sped forward. He crossed the 20 and cut sharply to the left. His bobblehead sprang forward as he changed directions, then recoiled back past his broad shoulders.

A trio of grim-faced Scorpions chased Zach in the backfield. Their bobbleheads bounced wildly as he tried to zigzag out of their clutches.

The Scorpion safety drove his elbow into the left side of Chris's head. Chris's bobblehead flew to the right, then rocketed back and smashed the safety's wooden helmet into a thousand splinters.

Zach spotted Chris speeding past midfield. He pulled his arm way, way back to fling the football as far as he could. But a Scorpion defender suddenly sunk his wooden teeth into the Lightning quarterback's arm.

Zach grimaced in pain and flipped the ball to his left hand. But another Scorpion chomped into that arm. Zach flipped the ball high in the air.

Chris was open and frantically waving his arms at Zach. He saw the football shooting high up above Zach and the Scorpion defenders. Then it plummeted back down.

His arms pinned and useless, Zach jerked his bobblehead back. His head sprang forward just as the football came down. Zach's fast-moving helmet struck the football, blasting it far downfield!

The football was sailing over Chris's head! He spun around and took off at warp speed. His bobblehead again trailed far behind as he sped after the ball. Chris stretched out his fingers and grabbed the football just as he crossed the goal line!

Zach's bobblehead shot backward after hitting the football. Its spring wrapped around and around the metal goal post.

The crowd was going nuts. Zach's teammates bounced their bobbleheads wildly as they celebrated the Mighty Bowl victory.

Zach wanted to join the celebration, but his head was hopelessly twisted around the goal post.

When Zach woke up, the sheets were twisted all around his body. He glanced at the row of bobbleheads standing at attention on the desk. Their heads were all jiggling and bouncing.

He blinked his eyes and looked again. The bobbleheads were all motionless.

Taking Care of Business

The Mighty Bowl kick-off was scheduled for noon, so Coach Mac had told Chris that he'd have to get an early start Saturday morning to finish the community service before the game.

There was a lot of territory to cover between the trailer park and the football field. It would have taken Chris four or five hours to do it. But Zach knocked on the trailer door at 7:45.

"Get your bike, amigo." Zach told his surprised friend. "We've got litter to clean up!"

Together, the boys rode their bikes up and down the streets of Westridge. Each had a large plastic trash bag tied to their handlebars.

The bags were full and the job was done by 9:30. When they rode their bikes onto the football field, they were the first ones there.

"Thanks a million, Zach! I don't think I could've finished in time without you."

"I'm just glad you're playing!" Zach really meant it. He knew the Lightning's chances of beating the Scorpions without Chris were practically zero. Not to mention the weight that was lifted from Zach's shoulders now that he didn't have to play quarterback.

Zach looked around the empty football field. "I wonder when the TV crew will get here."

"It's so cool the game's on TV!" Chris tossed the football to Zach.

"Only in Connecticut," Zach reminded him.

"You know how many people live in Connecticut? Millions!"

"Wow!"

"Millions of people watching us! Can you believe it, amigo?"

"We'll be famous!"

"Right!" Both boys were momentarily silent, lost in their dreams of glory. "If we win."

"If?!" Zach scoffed. "We're gonna destroy 'em, amigo!"

-27-
Ups and Downs

By the time their teammates started arriving, Zach and Chris had finished wind sprints, passing practice, and agility drills. They were sitting on the grass stretching their leg muscles when Dylan Yeager and Kelvin Jones approached.

"Chris!" Dylan and Kelvin both shouted as they saw their quarterback in his uniform.

Three more Lightning players ran up.

"You're playing, Chris?!" William Chen yelled.

Chris nodded, grinning broadly, as his teammates jumped on him, pummeling him excitedly. When the celebration was finally over, Lucas Higney scanned the field.

"Where's the TV cameras? I combed my hair in case they want to do a sideline interview!"

Everyone laughed loudly. Zach, though, was starting to worry. The game was in an hour. Maybe the TV crew wasn't coming after all.

Zach knew for sure there would be no TV crew at the Mighty Bowl when Coach Mac blew his whistle. It was time for the team's final huddle before the kick-off.

Zach was disappointed, of course. Not so much that millions of people in Connecticut wouldn't see the game, but that his dad wouldn't be watching and cheering him on. This was the biggest football game of his life! Zach needed his dad's support and encouragement now more than ever!

All the players in the huddle were excited, but nervous. Their palms were wet and their throats were dry.

"You're ready for this ballgame, boys. Everything you've learned this season has led you here."

Coach Mac's steady voice helped the boys calm down and focus.

"We're going to play our game, boys. The Scorpions can do whatever they want. If we play our game and give everything we have, we'll win."

The ref blasted his whistle to get the teams on the field for the kick-off.

Coach Mac paused to look at each of his players around the circle. "We're going to win the Mighty Bowl, boys."

He extended his right hand into the middle of the huddle. The boys all did the same, one hand on top of the other.

"One-Two-Three!" Coach Mac barked.

"Lightning!" The boys shouted louder than they ever had.

Surprise on the Sideline

Parents, brothers and sisters, grandparents, aunts and uncles, friends, neighbors, and other football fans were standing two-deep along both sidelines. They waved homemade signs and shouted encouragement to the players lining up for the kick-off.

Captain Dylan Yeager had called out "Heads!" when the ref tossed a silver dollar into the air. When it came up heads, Dylan chose to receive the kick-off.

Since Jared Greenberg was injured, Zach joined Chris as the Lightning kick returners. They stood on the 15-yard line, Chris on the left hash mark and Zach on the right. The other nine members of the Lightning return team spread out in front of them.

The ref handed the football to Dante Webb. As the Scorpion leader leaned down to place the ball on the kicking tee, Zach looked one last time at the sideline. Practically every parent held up a camera to record the action, but no TV crew was in sight.

The noise from the excited crowd was deafening, but Zach could hear Kate's high-pitched cheers.

"Go, Zach, go! Get 'em, Zach! Knock 'em down and run for a touchdown!"

Zach's eyes scanned the crowd in the direction of Kate's piercing shrieks. He spotted her jumping up and down and waving both her arms.

"Knock 'em down and run for a touchdown!"

Zach could see his mom beside Kate. She started to wave, but stopped and turned to look behind her.

"Ready to rock 'n roll, amigo?!" Chris called out. Zach smiled at his best friend and gave him a thumbs-up.

The Scorpions kick-off unit readied themselves. Dante took ten steps back, then turned to face the teed-up football.

Zach stole one last glance at the sideline. A man came up quickly behind his mom and grabbed her!

The ref blew his whistle and Dante started forward to kick the ball.

Zach's eyes were still riveted on the sideline. Instead of fighting the guy off, Zach's mom hugged him and they kissed! Zach blinked in disbelief. Then the guy leaned down and scooped Kate up into his arms.

It was his dad!

"Zach! Heads up!" Chris cried out.

Too late. The football hit Zach's knee and ricocheted back toward the oncoming Scorpions!

Luis Chavez and Austin Harrison dove for the bouncing ball. The Schwartz twins and three other Scorpion defenders dove for it at the same time.

More players jumped into the pile. There was a huge wrestling match at the 35-yard line as a dozen boys fought for the pigskin.

Zach and Chris stood and watched as the refs pulled the boys apart to see who was at the bottom of the pile with the football.

Chris glanced over at Zach and frowned. Zach was grinning ear to ear even though he had just messed up the opening kick-off.

"You okay?" Chris asked.

Zach couldn't speak. He just looked at Chris and kept grinning.

Lying at the bottom of the pile, crushed by over a thousand pounds of linemen, Marcus Newman held up the ball for everyone to see. The Lightning players all cheered as they pulled Marcus to his feet.

The wild fumble recovery energized the Lightning offense. Coach Mac kept the Scorpions defense off balance with a perfect mix of quarterback options and rollouts, quick slant passes, and fake and go routes up the seam.

Chris finished the drive with a spectacular 20-yard touchdown run. Six Scorpion tacklers grabbed nothing but air as Chris dodged and darted his way through the defense into the end zone.

Owen Carlson booted the extra-point between the goal posts to give the Lightning an early seven-point lead.

Unfortunately, Owen shanked the kick-off and the ball rolled out of bounds at the Lightning 41-yard line. Dante Webb didn't waste any time taking advantage of the great field position.

As amazing as Chris had been this season, Dante had been just as good. Of course, he had the advantage of being 13 years old while Chris was only 11. Dante was the only quarterback in the league who could match Chris's arm strength. And the Panthers' Rashard Thompson was the only kid in Westridge who could beat Dante in a race.

Dante's Scorpions had lost the Mighty Bowl two years in a row to the Lightning. He was determined to make his third and final year with the Scorpions end as the Mighty Bowl champions.

On first down, the Scorpion quarterback ran around left end for a 17-yard pick-up. With the ball on the 24, Dante pitched the ball back to the lone setback. The runner started right with a team of blockers in front of him.

All eleven Lightning defenders moved across the field toward the ball carrier. They didn't notice Dante slipping past them down the left sideline.

The Scorpion setback suddenly stopped and whirled around. He cocked his arm and sent a pass toward the left corner of the end zone.

The surprised Lightning defenders could only watch as the football sailed into the arms of Dante Webb in the end zone. Dante kicked the extra-point to tie the score at 7.

The Lightning offense continued clicking on their second possession of the game. William Chen dashed through a gaping hole created by Luis and Austin for a 12-yard gain. Chris faked a hand-off to Curtis Briggs, then rolled to the right and hit Connor Shaw in full stride.

The Scorpions cornerback dragged Connor down by his face mask at the 50. The ref threw his flag and signaled a 15-yard penalty against the Scorpion corner for the illegal tackle.

After William ran up the middle for a short gain, Chris again took to the air. He lofted the ball to Zach, who ran a perfect fade route.

Zach hauled in the pass over his shoulder and was pushed out of bounds at the Scorpions 26.

Zach skidded to a stop and looked up. Standing there above him was his father, smiling broadly and flashing a big thumbs-up.

"Dad!" Zach threw his arms around his father.

"Great to see you, son!"

The ref picked up the football and blew his whistle at Zach.

"Let's go, kid! The play clock's running!"

Zach couldn't let go of his dad. "But, Dad... How did you — !"

"I couldn't miss the Mighty Bowl, Zach! Now, get out there! Your team needs you!"

Mr. Fargo slapped the top of Zach's helmet. Zach grinned and raced full-speed back to the team's huddle.

On the next play, William took a hand-off from Chris and scooted for nine yards around left end.

On second and one at the Scorpions 17, Chris faked a hand-off to William and dropped back to pass. He pump-faked to Kelvin in the left flat, then turned and spotted Zach running a slant pattern across the middle.

The Scorpions strong safety saw that Zach was open. The safety leaned forward and sped directly at him.

Chris drilled the pass, hitting Zach between the numbers on the front of his jersey. But the safety crashed into Zach at that same moment.

The ball shot up into the air and fell into the hands of Dante Webb. Dante took the interception back 25 yards before Curtis tackled him at the 37.

Zach lay motionless at the five-yard line. His parents and the other fans on the Lightning sideline all held their breath.

Chris raced to Zach's side. "You okay, Zach?!"

Zach groaned and sat up. "I should've caught it."

"No, that was my fault. I shouldn't have thrown into that coverage."

Chris helped Zach to his feet. Coach Mac instructed Connor to sub for Zach at safety, but Zach waved him off.

"I'm okay, Coach!" To prove it, Zach sprinted to his safety position. He bounced up and down, eager to make up for the dropped pass.

As the other Scorpion and Lightning players trotted to their positions, Dalton Schwartz bumped into Zach.

"Nice catch, loser!" Dalton snorted, leaning in closer, his stinky breath in Zach's face. "You're gonna make this beatdown easy!"

Zach raised his hands to push the bully away.

"Zach!" Chris shouted.

Zach stopped, then took a step back, nodding at Chris.

"What's a matter?!" Dalton spoke in a mocking baby voice. "Baby want his mommy and daddy?" He laughed and started away. "Your parents are losers just like you!"

It was all Zach could do to keep from jumping on Dalton. If this had happened last year in the peewees, he would've jumped on him. He probably would've done a lot more than that. And then he would've been kicked out of the game and Dalton would have won.

But he kept it under control. Like Chris, Zach had learned a lot this season about football and about a whole lot more. Like how to man up when times were tough.

-29-
A Bloody Battle

The first quarter ended with the score knotted at 7. Dante Webb opened the second quarter by hitting his tight end on consecutive quick slants over the middle to move the ball to the Lightning 35.

On the next play of the drive, the Scorpions wide-out ran a hitch and go. He ran hard for six steps, paused like he was going to turn for a pass, then kicked it into high gear.

Curtis fell for the fake. When the wide-out blew past him, Curtis tried to recover, but slipped and fell at the 25.

With a quick flick of his wrist, Dante fired the ball to the wide open receiver. He didn't see Zach sprinting across the field.

The wide-out reached up for the pass at the five-yard line. But Zach flew in front of him and snatched the ball before the surprised wide-out could grab it.

Zach tucked the ball under his arm and turned upfield. He cut left and right, dodging tacklers. Max and Dalton Schwartz came at him, but Zach fooled them both with a quick stutter step. The twins crashed into each other and fell in a heap.

After throwing the interception, Dante had yanked off his chinstrap in frustration and waited for Zach to be brought down by one of the Scorpions upfield. When that didn't happen, he snapped his chinstrap back in place and took off to finish the job.

Not only was Dante the Scorpions MVP on offense, he was also their best tackler. He was the last Scorpion player with a chance to stop Zach.

Zach crossed the Scorpions 20-yard line. Out of the corner of his eye he saw number 14 racing across the field to cut him off. Zach veered toward the sideline, trying to get away from the Scorpions' speedy quarterback.

But Dante was closing the gap and Zach had to cut back at the ten to avoid running out of bounds. Dante lunged forward to grab Zach's legs. At that moment, Chris came flying out of nowhere and leveled Dante with a crushing block.

The crowd went nuts as Zach crossed the goal line. His 95 yard interception return for a touchdown was a Mighty Bowl record! Zach collapsed in exhaustion in the end zone as all of his teammates celebrated around him.

Owen kicked the extra-point and the Lightning regained the lead, 14-7.

The mark of a great competitor is not someone who wins every contest. It's a person who gets up every time they're knocked down. Who doesn't give up when things go wrong. A great competitor becomes even stronger when times are tough.

Dante Webb was a great competitor. Sure, he was a naturally gifted athlete, faster and stronger than most boys his age. But what made him a great football player was his will to win.

When the Scorpions lost those two Mighty Bowls, Dante became even more determined to never let that happen again. That's why he was always the first player at football practice and the last one to leave. That's why he lifted weights and ran wind sprints on hot summer days when other kids were playing at the pool.

That's why, when Chris flattened him on the five-yard line, Dante immediately jumped up and ran downfield to get ready to receive the next kick-off.

Those who knew the kind of competitor Dante was weren't surprised by what happened next. He took that kick-off, broke half a dozen tackles, and ran it back 80 yards for a touchdown!

The score was tied again, 14 to 14.

A quick touchdown can often trigger a change in momentum. A team that has been losing the battle at the line of scrimmage and trailing on the scoreboard can suddenly become filled with energy and confidence if they return a kick for a score.

But both teams just had quick scores. Zach's pick six and Dante's kick return balanced out. The two teams battled on.

Dante rocketed the kick-off all the way out of the end zone. The Lightning players hadn't seen anyone come close to that all year. Owen had a strong leg, but he was lucky if he could reach the 20-yard line.

On first down, the Lightning ran an off-tackle play for an eight-yard gain. That was the fourth time in the first half that William had followed the blocks of Luis and Austin for big yardage.

That was one thing about Coach Mac that surprised people. Everyone knew he had the biggest playbook in youth football. But he would run the same plays over and over if they were working.

On second down and two, he called another fade route. Zach cut toward the right sideline and made an over-the-shoulder catch for a 12 yard pickup and a first down.

The Lightning marched down the field, picking up five first downs. Kelvin ran a quick slant route, caught Chris's laser and split two defenders. He galloped all the way to the Scorpions six-yard line before both safeties brought him down.

Only 30 seconds remained in the half. The Lightning players hurried to huddle up.

"Nine Go Fade Right on one!" Chris told his teammates in the huddle.

"Jeez! What happened, Chris?" Zach cut in.

Everyone looked at Chris. Blood covered his mouth and chin.

"Somebody punched me."

Zach and the other Lightning players weren't surprised. Nothing the Scorpions did surprised them. But they were angry.

"Tell me which one hit you and I'll take care of him!" Parker hissed.

"Yeah, I'll help you!" normally-quiet Austin yelled, punching his palm with his fist.

"No!" Chris told them. "That's what they want us to do!"

Chris was right, and his teammates knew it. There was only one way to get back at the Scorpions. On the scoreboard!

The Lightning raced to the line. The clock ticked down to ten seconds. Across the line, Zach saw a red smear on Dalton Schwartz's silver jersey where he had wiped his bloody knuckles.

"Orange! 42!"

A ref's whistle blast cut off Chris's signals. The ref ran toward Chris for a closer look, then pointed to the sideline. League rules required that players who were bleeding had to leave the game until the bleeding was stopped.

The clock was stopped while Chris trotted off the field and Lucas Higney ran on. Zach was still lined up on the right side, ready to run the fade route that Chris had called.

Dylan Yeager looked over at Zach and called out, "You're the man, Fargo! Lucas is the wide-out!"

It took Zach a few seconds for Dylan's message to sink in. Chris was out of the game! Zach was the back-up quarterback!

His knees started to buckle. He took a deep breath, then raced to his new position in the shotgun behind center.

The ref blew his whistle and the clock started.

"Orange! 42! Hut!"

There was one second on the clock when Owen snapped the ball. Zach fumbled the snap, but quickly picked it up. The Scorpions front four crashed through the Lightning pass protection.

Zach looked for Lucas on the fade to the right, but Lucas was running across the middle. Realizing his mistake, Lucas turned and ran back to the right.

As the pass rushers tackled him, Zach heaved a pass to the right corner of the end zone. He was immediately buried under a pile of silver jerseys and couldn't see if Lucas caught the ball.

He didn't. The football sailed ten yards out of bounds. Dante Webb's grandpa, who was sitting in a lawn chair, caught Zach's pass.

-30-
The Fog Lifts

Kelvin's mom, the doctor, was still working on Chris's bloody mouth. All the other Lightning players swigged their water bottles as they gathered around Coach Mac.

"Great effort out there, boys. We left points on the field at the end of the half, but that was my fault. I should've called for a field goal."

"It's no one's fault, Coach," Zach said, still out of breath. "We win as a team, remember?"

Coach Mac nodded at Zach. "You're right, Zach. We win as a team."

"Unless I have to play quarterback again." Zach laughed, and the other boys joined in.

"Yeah, dude, that pass you threw looked like a wounded duck!" Lucas cracked.

"Don't insult the duck!" William added.

"Try using your right arm next time, Zach!"

"Better yet, tuck it and run!"

"No more passes! Please!"

Zach didn't mind the jokes. He was just relieved that he didn't have to play quarterback again. He almost choked on his water bottle because he was laughing so hard.

As the boys relaxed, Coach Mac walked over to check on Chris. Doctor Jones had cleaned up the blood on his face and had Chris biting on a gauze pad as she held an ice pack to his bottom lip.

"His lip needs stitches," the doctor told Coach Mac.

"Can it wait till after the game?"

"Yes. As long as he stays right here and doesn't open his mouth."

Chris pushed away the ice pack. "Buh, ah ga ah pah!" he protested through the mouthful of gauze. Chris tried to get up, but Coach Mac put a hand on his shoulder to keep him on the bench.

"I'm sorry, son. I know how much it means to you." But then Coach Mac winced in pain, putting his hand on his stomach.

"You better sit down, Coach," Doctor Jones told him.

Coach Mac shook his head. "It's nothing. Must be something I ate."

The Lightning players were back on their feet, eager for the second half to start. Coach Mac motioned for them to huddle up.

"Okay, boys, we start the half on defense. Owen takes Chris's spot at middle linebacker."

Everyone froze. That meant Chris wasn't playing!

"His lip is cut pretty bad," Coach Mac explained. "Chris is out for the rest of the game."

Coach Mac continued talking about defense and stopping Dante Webb and other important stuff, but Zach couldn't focus on what he was saying. That's because all of a sudden Zach felt dizzy. Everything was spinning around him in a blur. Even Coach Mac's words.

The Scorpions trotted out to their positions on the field. The ref blew his whistle to break the Lightning huddle.

"One-Two-Three!" Zach thought he heard Coach Mac's voice. Somewhere far off in the fog that surrounded Zach.

Every Lightning player in the huddle except Zach reached in to grab their coach's hand.

"Lightning!"

Owen ran forward and sent the second half kick-off sailing high into the air. The Lightning kick-off unit raced downfield as the football came down into the arms of Dante Webb.

Zach was still in a fog as he ran along behind his teammates. He had no idea where he was running. He was just following the others.

Suddenly, he smashed into a brick wall. A moving brick wall that appeared out of nowhere. Zach was knocked flat on his back. Max Schwartz smirked down at him.

And just like that, the fog surrounding Zach lifted. He looked up at Max and smiled.

"Thanks!" Zach jumped to his feet and sprinted downfield.

Austin Harrison tackled Dante at the 40. Zach raced up and clapped Austin on the back.

"Way to go, Big A! Alright, guys! Let's get the ball back!"

Zach was totally pumped up. And the other Lightning players started picking up on his energy.

"Yeah! Let's shut 'em down!"

"Three and out!"

The second half of the biggest game of his life had started! And Zach couldn't wait to give it everything he had to give.

A New Leader

Strong safety Marcus Newman blitzed on first down and blind-sided Dante Webb. Dante was much bigger, but Marcus used one of his wrestling moves to bring Dante to the turf for a ten-yard loss.

On the next play, Luis Chavez broke up a screen pass in the left flat.

On third and 20, the Scorpions QB hit his favorite wide-out on a crossing pattern. It would have been a first down, but Zach crashed into the receiver, jarring the ball loose. William Chen fell on the fumble and it was Lightning ball!

Zach pulled William up and gave him a double high-five.

"Great play, William!"

"Hey, you're the one who made the play! All I did was fall on the ball."

Zach didn't see it that way. Leaders don't focus on themselves because they're focused on everyone around them. That's what makes them great leaders. And that's what Zach was quickly becoming.

As the Lightning players huddled up, Zach looked to the sideline to get the play. But he didn't see Coach Mac. Zach looked left and right, craning his neck, but Coach Mac wasn't there!

Zach turned back to his teammates in the huddle. They waited for him to tell them the play Coach Mac had called. Zach hesitated for a moment. If his teammates figured out that their new quarterback was lost, they'd have no chance of winning the Mighty Bowl.

"Wing Right 24 Dive on three." Zach said it like nothing was wrong. Like Coach Mac had signaled the play to him.

The Lightning broke huddle and charged to the line. Although Zach hadn't had much time to come up with a play, he'd made a wise choice. He'd called a simple running play that didn't have much chance of ending in disaster.

Zach took the snap and handed it to William Chen. Luis and Austin opened up a hole on the right side and William scooted through for a first down.

Zach looked again to the sideline. Coach Mac was nowhere to be seen. Lucas Higney was standing there, though, frantically waving his hands back and forth. Zach had no idea what Lucas was trying to tell him.

Zach called three more running plays that gained a total of five yards. The Scorpion defense was clamping down on the run, figuring the sub at QB wasn't going to throw the ball.

It was fourth down with five yards to go for a first down. The ball was at the Scorpions 25 yard line. Too far for Owen to try a field goal. Too close to punt.

Zach knew another running play would probably come up short. He was going to have to call a pass play.

"Left Slant Nine Go on two." Zach tried to sound confident, but he kept thinking about his last pass to Dante's grandpa in the lawn chair.

Zach took a deep breath as he stood behind Owen and called out the signals. "Mike! Red! 42! Hut!"

He took the snap, stepped back, and lofted a pass over the middle linebacker to Kelvin.

The tall tight end reached up and grabbed the ball without breaking stride. He brushed off two defenders and turned upfield.

A cornerback jumped on Kelvin, but Kelvin just kept running. He crossed the goal line with the cornerback hanging on his back!

Zach had his first touchdown pass, but he wasn't thinking about that. The Lightning again had the lead! Owen's extra-point kick made the score 21-14.

As the two teams trotted downfield to line up for the kick-off, Zach raced to the sideline.

"Where's Coach?!"

"I don't know!" Marcus Newman pulled on his helmet and started onto the field.

Zach looked at Doctor Jones. "Have you seen Coach Mac?!"

"He's not feeling well." She nodded in the direction of the portable toilets lined up behind the end zone.

Zach couldn't believe it. Not only was he playing quarterback in the Mighty Bowl, but with Coach Mac gone, Zach had to do all the play calling.

Even pro QB's didn't call their own plays. They all had coaches up in the pressbox who made those decisions.

"Hey, Za! Ni—Pa–!" Chris yelled through the cotton in his mouth.

Zach thought Chris had tried to say, "Nice Pass!" but he wasn't sure. He looked at his best friend sitting on the bench, head tilted back and an ice pack on his mouth. Chris lifted his right arm and gave Zach a thumbs-up.

That was exactly what Zach needed at that moment. Chris believed Zach could do it. Why shouldn't Zach believe it too?

-32-
Down But Not Out

The third quarter ended with Dante Webb scoring on an electrifying run from the Lightning 40. After scrambling away from Marcus Newman on a blitz, Dante stiff-armed Dylan, the Lightning's best tackler. Dante then reversed direction and plowed over the Lightning secondary.

Zach, Curtis, and William Chen were all left sprawled on the ground as Dante scored. His extra-point kick tied the game at 21.

Then, disaster struck on the Lightning's first play of the fourth quarter. Zach rolled out on an option and, when the Scorpions defensive end came at him, he pitched the ball to William Chen.

But the Scorpions outside linebacker cut between Zach and William and intercepted the lateral. He cruised into the end zone untouched to give the Scorpions their first lead of the game. Dante booted the extra-point to make the score 28-21.

At that point in the game, it would have been easy for the Lightning players to hang their heads and give up. The momentum had clearly shifted in favor of the Scorpions. If the Scorpions scored again, it would be impossible for the Lightning to come back.

Dylan Yeager could see the game slipping away. As the captain, he felt responsible for keeping everybody positive.

"Let's go, guys! We can do it!" he pumped his fist, trying to get his teammates to believe it.

But sometimes words are not enough. Some-times it takes action. And that's what Zach was planning as he waited at the ten yard line for Dante's kick-off.

"William!" he called over to William Chen, who had taken Chris's spot as the other deep returner. "If I get the ball, run to the sideline! And stay behind me!"

William wasn't sure what Zach was planning, but he nodded anyway.

The kick-off sailed end over end into Zach's arms. He started upfield along the right hash marks. The Scorpions all charged at him.

Suddenly, Zach stopped running. He turned and fired the ball all the way across the field to

William, who was standing next to the left side-line.

The only thing the Scorpions could do was watch as William scooted up the sideline 70 yards for a touchdown. Owen drilled the extra-point kick and the score was tied 28-28.

Just like that, the Lightning players regained their positive attitude. Win or lose, Zach was determined they kept it.

Zach told Owen to try a short squib kick instead of booting the kick-off downfield to Dante Webb again.

The plan caught the Scorpions off-guard. Owen's kick ricocheted off Max Schwartz' leg and bounced toward the sideline. Lucas Higney dove for the ball, but it skidded out of bounds at the Scorpions 12-yard line.

The Scorpions were 88 yards away from the end zone and only five minutes remained in the final quarter. If the Lightning could stop the Scorpions, then get the ball back and score, the Mighty Bowl championship would be theirs!

Dante Webb called his team into the huddle and told them exactly what was going to happen.

"We're gonna march down the field, eat up the clock, and score! We have 'em right where we want 'em!"

Zach figured the Scorpions wouldn't want to leave any time on the clock if they scored. He decided to blitz on first down and hope Dante didn't throw a long pass.

His gamble worked. Dante took the snap and started right on a sweep. He didn't see Zach coming from behind him.

Zach blasted Dante between the shoulders and the football popped free. It bounced out of bounds at the Scorpions six yard line.

Zach blitzed again on second down. But this time Dalton Schwartz saw him coming and stuck out his leg and tripped him.

Dante had plenty of time in the pocket to look downfield and see his wide-out run by Curtis. With Zach lying on the ground at the line of scrimmage instead of helping out in pass coverage, the receiver was wide open.

Dante fired a perfect pass and the wide-out took it the rest of the way for a 94-yard touchdown.

Except there was a yellow flag on the ground. The ref had seen Dalton trip Zach and threw the flag. The touchdown pass was called back.

The ref moved the football back to the three-yard line. The Scorpions were eating up the clock, but they were marching backwards!

Owen Carlson nearly ended the Scorpions drive on the next play. Dante threw a quick pass over the middle to his tight end.

Owen, who was playing middle linebacker in place of Chris, saw the ball coming straight at him. He didn't have time to think about it. The pass sailed right into his hands.

But instead of running with it, or wrapping his arms around it and falling to the ground, Owen just stood there and stared at the football in amazement.

The Scorpions tight end ripped the ball out of Owen's hands. The receiver took off running and Marcus tackled him at the 35.

"Owen!" Dylan was angry, but stopped himself. "Next time just fall on it!"

Owen nodded, but hung his head, embarrassed by his mistake.

Zach slapped him on the back. "No one takes the blame on our team!"

The Scorpions tried to hustle to the line of scrimmage before the Lightning could regroup.

Dante ran around left end for a 20-yard pick-up. Without stopping to huddle, he ran a quarterback draw up the middle. It looked like Dante was going to break free, but Owen charged at him and knocked him backwards five yards.

The ref blew his whistle to stop play for the two-minute warning. Both teams went to their sidelines for water and a final huddle with the coaches.

Coach Mac was standing there when the Lightning players arrived.

"Coach is back!"

"Alright!"

"Are you okay, Coach?"

Coach Mac waved off their questions. "I'm fine. But I can't believe I left my playbook in there." He looked at the portable toilets.

The boys all laughed.

"Looks like you boys have done just fine without me. I'm not surprised. I knew you would.

Now all you have to do is stop them and we'll win it in overtime."

"We didn't do it without you, Coach." Zach spoke for all of the boys. "You were there with us the whole time."

Coach Mac looked at Zach and nodded. He knew he had two leaders on the team now. One was sitting over there with an ice pack on his face. The other was Zach.

Coach Mac held out his right hand.

"One-Two-Three."

"Lightning!"

Coach Mac's boys raced back onto the field to make a final stand. The Scorpions were already waiting for them.

Dante took the snap and dropped back to pass. Dylan blew past his blocker and charged at the Scorpions QB. But Dante ducked and Dylan flew right over him.

Straightening up, Dante spotted his running back alone in the flat. The running back caught Dante's pass and started upfield. He dodged Lucas Higney, but was knocked out of bounds by Curtis at the 15-yard line.

Again the Scorpions lined up without huddling. Dylan yelled the defensive signals as the Lightning defenders hurried into position.

Dante ran straight ahead for five yards. On second and five, he bulled his way up the middle for six more yards and a fresh set of downs.

The clock kept running. 40 seconds, 39, 38…

Everyone knew Dante was going to run up the middle again and again until he scored. But it didn't matter if everyone knew. No one could stop him.

Three Lightning linemen wrestled Dante down at the one. On second and goal, Dylan and Luis hit Dante at the line of scrimmage, but Dante refused to go down. His legs kept churning until he pushed his way across the goal line.

The touchdown gave the Scorpions a six point lead. Dante's extra-point kick made it 35-28.

Only 12 seconds remained on the clock. The Lightning players could only watch in silence as the Scorpions celebrated.

Double Flea Flicker With Extra Sprinkles

Zach knew there was only one way for the Lightning to tie the game and get into overtime. They had to run the kick-off back for a touchdown.

Twice this season, Chris had taken kick-offs to the house. But not Zach. And he knew he couldn't try that cross-field throw to William again because the Scorpions would be looking for it.

Zach didn't get a chance to return the kick-off. Dante booted it all the way out of the end zone. The ref placed the football on the 20-yard line. The Lightning had 80 yards to go and time for only one more play.

Zach looked to the sideline to get the play from Coach Mac. At first, Zach didn't understand the complicated signal. Then he nodded. The play Coach Mac signaled to him was exactly the one he was hoping it would be!

The Lightning players in the huddle were silent. Zach knew from the gloomy looks on their faces that their hopes for victory were gone.

"Double Flea Flicker With Extra Sprinkles, on one." Zach couldn't hide his smile as he

147

announced the play. The other boys looked up at him. Double Flea Flicker With Extra Sprinkles! They started smiling too as their hope returned. The Mighty Bowl wasn't over yet!

A flea flicker is a trick play in which the quarterback hands the ball to a running back who fakes a run up the middle, then turns and tosses the ball back to the quarterback. As the defense moves up to stop the run, the QB throws a long bomb to a wide-open receiver. Most teams have a version of the flea flicker in their playbook. They might call it once or twice a season.

The Double Flea Flicker With Extra Sprinkles took that trick play and made it a whole lot trickier. Coach Mac was the only coach in the country who had the Double Flea Flicker With Extra Sprinkles in his playbook. And he had never used it in a game before.

"Hot Fudge! 86! Down! Hut!" Zach barked out the signals. The clock started when Owen hiked the ball.

Zach took the snap and handed the football to William Chen. William took two steps up the middle, then turned and tossed the ball back to Zach. That's when the extra sprinkles began.

Instead of looking downfield for a receiver, Zach turned and threw an overhand lateral to Curtis, who was standing next to the right sideline. Curtis caught the ball and started running.

The Scorpions defense shifted over to tackle Curtis. But Curtis suddenly stopped at the 35-yard line. He turned and threw an overhand lateral back to Zach. Zach was standing at the 30 because he had moved upfield while Curtis was running.

All the Scorpions stopped in their tracks and started running back in the opposite direction. Zach then turned left and threw another overhand lateral. This time Connor Shaw caught it along the left sideline.

While football rules allow only one forward pass per play, a team can do as many backward passes or laterals as it wants. The regular old flea flicker has one backward lateral. The Double Flea Flicker With Extra Sprinkles had six.

Connor tucked the football under his arm and ran forward to the 50-yard line. The Scorpions thought he was heading for the end zone, so they ran all the way across the field to stop him.

Connor suddenly stopped and threw a backward pass to Zach, who was waiting at the 45.

The exhausted Scorpions again reversed direction. Max and Dalton Schwartz gave up. They were bent over at midfield, trying to catch their breath.

Dante Webb was the only Scorpion defender who wasn't fooled by the Double Flea Flicker With Extra Sprinkles. When Curtis had thrown the ball back to Zach, and all the other Scorpions ran back in that direction, Dante stayed next to Curtis.

"It's not gonna work, kid." Dante figured the ball would be coming back to Curtis. And he wanted to be there to intercept the lateral and end the game.

Zach again turned to the right to throw the football over to Curtis. That was supposed to be lateral number six. But Dante was there, waiting.

Zach looked downfield and saw Kelvin Jones wide open in the end zone. But Zach had crossed the line of scrimmage, so a pass from where he was standing would be illegal.

Zach knew he was holding the ball too long. He was right. Two Scorpion defenders hit him from opposite sides and the football popped up high in the air.

Zach tried to reach up for it, but one Scorpion had his left arm and the other Scorpion had his right.

Out of the corner of his eye, Zach spotted William Chen moving in to try and block for him.

Zach swung his head and batted the falling football with his helmet. Just like the bobbleheads always did in his dreams!

The ball sailed into William's hands! William sped toward the right sideline, but that's where Dante Webb was waiting. Dante started forward to make the tackle.

William had nowhere to go. He couldn't keep going right because he would run out of bounds. He turned back to the left, but the Scorpion defenders who had hit Zach were coming at full speed. William had no choice but try to somehow run over the much larger Dante Webb.

Just as William and Dante were about to collide, a tiny blur shot between them, knocking Dante off balance.

As Dante fell, William stepped around him and starting running down the sideline. Dante sat there surprised and looked to see who had leveled him.

Curtis pushed his glasses back on his nose and grinned.

The Lightning parents started jumping up and down and cheering as William crossed the 40, the 30, the 20.

The exhausted Scorpions could do nothing but watch as William sped into the end zone.

The fans along the Scorpions sideline were too stunned to speak. They couldn't believe what they had just seen.

All the Lightning players raced into the end zone to celebrate. They pounded each other on the back and danced crazily.

Zach seemed to be the only one who knew the game wasn't over.

"Guys! Line up! We don't want a penalty!"

Although no time was left on the clock, the game still had one more play – the extra-point. And if Owen Carlson kicked the football through the uprights, the score would be tied at 35-35 and the Mighty Bowl would have its first ever overtime game!

Zach knelt at the ten-yard line to await the snap. It was his job to catch the ball and quickly stand it on the ground for Owen to kick it. Since Owen was the team's regular center, Parker Coates hiked the ball for all the extra-point kicks.

The three boys had spent a lot of time practicing the hikes, holds, and kicks. And their hard work had paid off. Owen made 20 of 22 extra-point kicks during the season.

Maybe it was the excitement of the Double Flea Flicker With Extra Sprinkles, or maybe it was nervousness, but Parker hiked the ball over Zach's head. Not only over Zach's head, but also over Owen, who was standing five yards behind Zach.

The football bounced all the way back to the 25-yard line!

Owen stood there, unsure what to do. A trio of Scorpions ran over him as they chased after the ball. But Zach beat them to it.

As soon as he saw the football sailing over his head, Zach had sprung to his feet. He flew past Owen and scooped up the bouncing ball. But as he turned, he saw the three Scorpions charging straight at him.

Zach started running in the wrong direction, away from the end zone. He ran all the way back to the 40, then turned in a wide arc and sped around the three Scorpion linemen.

Zach crossed the 30, the 25, the 20. A second wave of Scorpions was coming at him.

As he ran, Zach raised the ball in his right hand and pointed to the end zone with his left. He pointed first to the left, then to the right, as if signaling his receivers.

The Scorpion defenders thought he was going to pass, so they all turned to see which player they needed to guard. But there weren't any Lightning players in the end zone.

As the Scorpions turned back toward him, Zach crossed the five and dove for the goal line. Dante Webb and three other Scorpions hit him in mid-air.

Zach landed underneath them all. With his face pressed against the grass, he could see that he was lying inches short of the goal line.

The refs pulled the Scorpions off the pile. At the bottom lay Zach on the one-yard line.

But his arms were extended out in front of him. And in his hands was the football.

Zach's body hadn't crossed the goal line, but the football had!

Both refs raised their arms to the sky, signaling that Zach had scored two points!

The Lightning had defeated the Scorpions 36-35! They were the Mighty Bowl champions!

-34-
Two Wins

The Lightning players and their families hung around the field for a long time after the game. No one wanted to have the incredible experience end.

"Curtis, you laid Dante Webb out!" Two hundred pound Dylan Yeager nearly knocked little Curtis over with a high five. "When did you learn to block like that?!"

"I don't know," Curtis was beaming ear to ear. "I just did it!"

"Hey, Parker!" Lucas called out. "What was up with that last snap? It looked like you were trying to split the uprights at the other end of the field!"

"Yeah," Parker giggled, "Guess I was a little too pumped up!"

Kelvin stood before them all, waving his arms like a music conductor. "Hey, Lightning! What's your favorite ice cream topping?"

"Extra sprinkles!" they all shouted.

Coach Mac stood to one side, happy for the boys, and impressed with their amazing show of strength and determination in the Mighty Bowl.

They were definitely on their way to becoming fine young men.

Coach Mac knew his job was done. At least until next season.

Finally, Doctor Jones insisted that Chris had to go get the stitches put in his lip. Chris punched knuckles with all his teammates as Mrs. Rivera and Doctor Jones took him away.

"Way t' go, Za–!" Chris's swollen lip made it hard for him to talk.

Zach gave his best friend a big hug. "I couldn't have done it without you, amigo!"

The other Lightning players slowly drifted off, until only Zach and his family remained.

"Boy, am I glad I didn't miss that game!" said Mr. Fargo. "I've never seen anything like it!"

"Yes, it was a miracle," added Mrs. Fargo. "The game and you being here." She smiled and gave her husband a kiss.

"What was your favorite part, Kate?" Zach asked his little sister, who was cuddling in her father's arms.

"The Daddy being here part!" Then Kate quickly added, "But I liked your football part too!"

"You know, Zach, I have to apologize for making everyone think the TV crew would be here. They would've been, but my boss decided I could come home early."

"That's okay, Dad," Zach answered. "I'm just glad you were able to come back for the weekend!"

"Zach," his mom said, "your father said he came home early."

"Huh?" Zach looked confused for a moment, then his eyes grew wide with excitement. "You mean, you don't have to go back to Connecticut, Dad?!"

"That's right, son."

Zach leaped up and hugged all three of them. "We did it! We won!"

"Won what?" asked Kate.

"Dad being gone! We won that too!"

As Zach and his family walked back to the parking lot, Mr. Fargo held up his phone.

"I just sent the Mighty Bowl to the guys I worked with."

"Dad, that's kind of embarrassing," Zach moaned. "They've probably never even heard of the Mighty Bowl."

"No, Zach. They watched all the games your mom sent to me. You may not realize it, but you have a lot of fans in Connecticut!"

"For real, Dad?"

"For real, son."

"Wow!" Kate squealed. "My brother's famous! Maybe they'll make a bobblehead of Zach!"

And everyone laughed.

404951R00101

Made in the USA
Lexington, KY
22 April 2016